Rebel Angels Down in Texas

I0566671

Martin O'Hurley

San Gabriel Publishing
Georgetown TX
2016

Thanks to my outstanding editor Sandy; great advice from Monique; Michelle with a sharp eye, and Sundie for keeping me from starving.

Guardian angels of life sometimes fly so high as to be beyond our sight, but they are always looking down upon us.

Jean Paul Richter

Then they heard a loud voice from The heaven saying to them, "Come up here." And they went up to heaven in a cloud, while their enemies looked on.

Revelation 11:12

Any sufficiently advanced technology is indistinguishable from magic.

Arthur C. Clarke

Rebel Angels Down in Texas

Angel in the Basement
1

See the great man.

He swivels in the battered black chair, as much duct tape as chair. It is dawn on a Saturday in the perpetual summer of late 2099. He swivels in the steeple round room atop a very old Mission just outside of Forth Worth. Formerly Texas. The Mission is white adobe and would be called plain if not for the solar panels and unusual cross on the dome above him. The cross came with the Mission but the steel orb at the peak was his doing. A Mission girded for the times. His eleven mates simply call it the Church.

The round room is of modest diameter, modified to serve as a sentry tower. A necklace of porthole windows rim the wall at chair viewing level. They portholes are nautical, with thick glass round-framed by bolt heads to preserve a semblance of coolness against a hammer of a sun.

The walls are wrapped in shiny foil insulation held in place by chicken wire and thin wood strips in tent frame fashion. The floor is black timbers with gapped joints long shed of their mud grout, creating a grate for air flow. Evaporative coolers in the basement push air up a clear bank drive-through tube he pulled from a First Command branch not far.

He rolls the tired chair a little to get in the tube stream. Air ruffles the sleeves of his green vacation style shirt with impossibly green parrots. Two screwdriver heads peek from his cargo pant pocket. Red Roman sandals that probably sat gathering dust on a shelf in Fort Worth for decades scuff back and forth on the timbers. He needed coffee. Nik and Mari would be up in a bit to have a pot and talk about the visuals. But the first look was his duty. He dreaded it every morning.

Fingers tapping the grimy tape arms. Camo binoculars hang from one, twisting. Staring intently across a sea of sand. The chair complains with that addictive squeak that forces one to swivel.

His panorama takes in the desert known as the Scald to the south and burned up Forth Worth to the north. Later he will check the north. On the far edge of the once huge metroplex a tire fire has burned since 84'. He watches the black undulating funnel dance every day. Nik says it looks like a belly dancer.

First light means eyes on the Scald, looking for stray Hags, or worse.

Sara was tapping out coffee grounds downstairs so wouldn't be long.

A flock of birds was growing larger in the portholes. Black-Capped Vireos. Should be in Mexico by now, the opposite direction. Birds had been confused for a couple weeks now and he had no idea why. They drafted and soared over the Church, causing the portholes to blink.

He asked Angel for the visual from Hagtown. Angel lived in the basement, with her own small room between the coolers and the powerwall 10 batteries and above the water pumps. Her technical name was Angel Q1, his prototype Quantum built before the collapse. Angel Q1 backed up the

Internet on January 1 2058 as the Water Wars loomed. While his colleagues escaped with meagers he carried the little black cylinder through an inferno and then a deluge. Angel and the clothes on his back. He missed his wife and baby so much. Seventeen years. The first years were...difficult. Hiding from Hag scouts while working on the Stealth. Fighting for food and eating almost anything. Hags looting and burning everything. Nik and Mari scrounging for supplies and protecting him and the others.

He ruminated on these things while Angel ran a hologram. The opening visual was always a fast glide over the Scald. When the town came into view he was looking for certain things and would try to block out atrocities. Groups of soldiers with battle straps up would get his attention. Body parts being hacked off would not. Columns of men moving out of the gate north would get him out of his chair.

His motley fleet of solar drones did not have night vision, thus early light was most critical. The Scald was flat and wide and provided a good line-of-sight video feed.

The Church had an important edge. The horde of twelve thousand to the south could not see them. His large scale Stealth was theoretical for most of the century; but necessity was the mother of invention and he found a way when all hope was fading. In the world before he would have won a Nobel. Angel used a laser to refresh a matrix of visual transcriptors every minute, exactly. For the twelve this was a clockwork silent blue laser that was the heartbeat of the Church. For all others the Church was more desert.

This Saturday morning on the last day of October was typical. A glide over the Scald looking for columns or strays, once around the perimeter fence, then visuals on the house of the boss. The boss was the man himself, Harold Hag the giant, his castle a circa 2020 two story on a cul de sac in the center of the town bearing his name. Congealed might be a better description for the population. His boys Franklin and Levi were the only other houses on the round, all others having been razed to clear a dead zone for the uninvited.

The drone circled five hundred feet above the giant. The razor wire atop his cyclone fence was free of bloody arms or legs, thus a sedate evening at the Hag residence. The plywood windows in back had cook smoke drifting from the battle slits. The low bricks had a mud plaster forged by the hammer sun. A sacrifice altar in front of a spit over a fire pit was back of the lot where seventy years ago kids were playing in a sprinkler on a nice green lawn with nice parents talking to nice neighbors.

He had seen this house, this scene, thousands of times. But something was different today. His burred hair was tingling alive in that moment your lizard brain knows something before you know it. He asked Angel to zoom to a reflection from a window on the top floor facing north. Three windows, two plywood and one glass, with the glass in the middle. It was new. Wasn't there yesterday. A figure was in the hall behind the glass.

The figure stepped to the window.

He came out of his chair.

This cannot be.

Light in the Dark

2

The dream was replayed not every night, but often. I lay awake after one of them.

Seventeen years ago, when she was seventeen. I had gone scrounging for grub when the Hags had rolled into Fort Worth, inspired to kill democracy dead-enders after a hellfire sermon from the giant at the Hag's annual God and Guns barbecue. The barbecue turned out to be the dead-enders, several thousand of whom were being herded into large parking lots to be culled.

The lot I was watching surrounded a long abandoned mega-church. The huge asphalt lake had long ago lost the white parking stripes and was a black lava blob with grass poking through in frequent clumps. The edges had flea-market vendor stalls. Church pews had been stacked man-high in a sunken section of the blob, then set ablaze using hymnals and not-Harold-approved Bibles for kindling. The pew shellac put off a noxious smoke that didn't seem to bother the Hags. The heat was tremendous, buckling asphalt and setting stalls on fire. The dead-enders had been herded to the opposite end of the parking lot at the points of hundreds of blades in the hands of very scary men. Lambs huddled together.

A very psychotic-looking Hag was singing Amazing Grace into the fire at the barely tolerable edge of the heat. His head was split down the middle with long matted hair on one side and shaved smooth on the other. The smooth had a big red scorpion tattoo that looked like a cross with curled ends. The roaring flames and his dramatic rendition had the scorpion dancing. His mates were backing up with a pew and knocked him stumbling head down nearly into the inferno. The long greasy hair swung out and caught fire like a match head as he jerked back. He was spinning across the asphalt like a scorpion fire dervish to roars of laughter. He sprinted past the lambs and fell down almost out of sight on the dark edges of the lot, smoking. His mates went about their business. I remember thinking how did these people fall down this bad.

I had watched from behind a Hag wagon with a machete and a fillet blade pulled from the cook's wagon right after slipping it into the cook's ear.

A big man I later knew as Franklin Hag had been trying to administer some sort of loyalty oath to find the atheists among the herd, presumably to be eaten first. He was yelling something about science and liberals and had men pulling crying children away from screaming parents. When the fire dervish spun by he laughed and seemed to lose interest in his speech and turned and yelled cook them all.

Mari was pulled from the grasp of a man who must have been her Father and slapped as she jerked back, knocked out. A slap of good fortune to be unconscious, doubly so to fall in view of Franklin, who turned to his aid de camp and nodded towards the wagon behind the cook. I watched from behind the wagons' wheel as the big Hag pulled her by the hair across the asphalt.

She stirred conscious from the pain, her screams mimed against the screams of the slaughter of the lambs. I lopped off his right hand as he reached to lay down the wagon gate, blood spurting into his face as he looked at where his hand used to be. He dropped her hair with his left and looked at me wide-eyed and slack-jawed, then down at his hand on the asphalt. I stepped back then forward whipping the blade into his open mouth, removing his lower jaw and coming to rest in the top of his throat.

He fell to his knees and I pulled the blade out with my right boot on what remained of his head while pulling her roughly with my left hand to clear his sagging bulk. She was awake but in shock, wide-eyed and shivering as I pulled her along behind the cover of the Hag wagon train into darkness down the boulevard moving southwest. The screams could not fade fast enough. We secreted in a stand of Texas Bluegrass on a hillside outside of the city proper. I held her all night as she shivered, telling her to look at me, focus on me, it will be all right. We lit out before dawn to my secure little bunker in an old Catholic Mission on the north edge of the Scald.

———————————

She stirred, mumbling into my shoulder blade about wearing her out last night. I could feel her smile as I smiled, feeling cocksure of myself as she traced her finger over a shoulder scar and up my neck to the edge of a fresh burr cut, giving me a shiver. She blew on my neck to make it worse.

Shouldn't you have a zipper on your neck?

I did a sheet tangling roll into her warm body, kissing her teeth in smile then her lips in moan. We had that early morning lovers smell that was heady and hot but flirting with not. Hand down her smooth belly to her hip, pulling her in tighter. The nylon mat on my knuckles and her ass on my palm, kissing her neck, tasting her. Her hair always seemed to smell like Texas Bluegrass. I looked into her green eyes just as the days first sun ray cut the portholes, converging into a sunburst across her face. She caressed my face with both hands, pulling me back in.

Afterward I paced the portholes, checking for movement. Our little cubicle was the front southeast corner of the Church, first line of defense against the Hags. The Church had ten cubicles in the nave, a big dining table in the sanctuary, and a kitchen on the altar. The tabernacle had a nice flat surface perfect for cutting yams and potatoes. I knew at this moment Dr. B was upstairs looking south, steeling himself for the morning hologram. I heard tin cups clink in the kitchen as Sara got their morning strong brew. In one of the greatest scrounge jackpots of all time Mari had uncovered a semi-trailer full of coffee beans sitting in some trees on an old golf course out by Willow Creek. We didn't know how it got there and didn't care. We hauled coffee for weeks and now spent our days properly amped.

Mari set tin cups on our little wood table and the coffee was starting to perc on the solar stove. The laser crossed the portals and hit the sand with a red white and blue display that reminded me of the old pledge of allegiance.

While she poured coffee, I went to the sanctuary and pulled the mission bell clapper down and slipped it into a notch in the altar. We called it the Hail Mary chain as it was attached to a counterweight on the ceiling used to open and close the hail doors for the solar panels. It was still Texas after all.

Sara was on her way upstairs with a hot pot and said good morning. She was in good spirits. Her and Dr B were sometimes an item. They were originals, survivors of the Water Wars in 58 and all the hell that followed. The sinking ship of civilization had tossed loved ones overboard no matter how hard you held them. I liked seeing her happy.

I hurried back, bare feet on the stone floor, the morning air cool on my burr. The other cubicles were coming to life.

I leaned against the adobe sipping a cup, feeling the heat building on my lower back. The cool basement air gently soothed my bare chest. The whoosh of the bank tube was a comforting sound. I propped a foot against the adobe to feel the bake. The coffee steam swirled and eddied. Sunlight diffused room. Looked like Bladerunner. Mari was bathed in gold steam sitting at our battered little table. She sideways glanced me, taking a sip.

Breakfast was simple, a combination of potatoes and whatever protein we had scrounged from supply forays into the metroplex. Six months ago, we had discovered a cache of protein powder in a gym down in Burleson, buried under pile of fitness detritus the Hags had no use for. The gym supply room was a basement, the cool temps preserving the powder nicely. I took a bite of carrot and chased it with mocha mint mixed in water.

She was watching me. She two handed sipped her cup.

You like that mocha mint. I should call you
      mocha boy.

I think I'm more like your pool boy.

She laughed and nudged me under the table.

Careful that's your whole world there.

Oh god you are so full of yourself.

A minute ago you were full of me too, said with a wink.

She gave me her biggest grin with the double eyebrow raise.

She's in a black crop top and black yoga pants. She liked yoga pants and I liked them too. On her. Hags sought out anything deemed technology to burn, so certain desirable things could still be found. There had to be some luck, as with our coffee trailer and gym powder. We had that luck last month when we uncovered a trove of women's active wear from a strip mall in Grapevine turned upside down by a tornado. She was giggling like a schoolgirl as we hauled back all sorts of colorful stretchy things. I liked them all. On her.

I checked the portholes again. The stone floor had discolored into a path that if we lived to one hundred would be a trench. For some strange reason, it reminded me of a very old Monty Python bit with priests or monks or something walking around banging their heads with tablets while chanting.

We discussed the agenda even though we didn't need to.

Angel gives us todays agenda.

Meet with Dr B for debriefing and coffee. An hour of blade training followed by a security sweep. A quick cold shower then something to eat while Dr B held a math class, followed by an hour of short blade training and an hour of heat training in the Mood suits. Another cold shower and some rest. Plan for our next scrounge.

We had supper on the altar at six followed by social time. We rotated a set of eyes in the sentry tower at all times from sunup to sundown. Everybody got an hour every day.

At dark, we put our faith in Angel and the Stealth.

We were discussing what might be for supper when Sara rapped on the door and stuck her head in. I knew something was up from her rapid patter down the stairs.

Need you guys upstairs she said.

I grabbed a t-shirt and we hurried up behind her. Dr B was in his chair, elbows on the arms, head down. Sara kneeled beside him and put a hand on his arm.

Good morning kids he said without looking up. He always called us kids when we were together.

Mari kneeled in front of him and put her hand on his cheek.

Are you ok? What has happened?

He took her hand and kissed it and held it in his lap.

Well quite a surprise I must say dear girl. This morning's hologram had a big surprise.

He looked up at me.

We had seen many terrible things in Hagtown. The depths of the dark heart. When someone who had watched sadistic cannibals for nearly seventeen years was this upset - that could not be good.

Before you see this, I want you to know something. Your blood will be up and you will be ready for battle. But we must discuss it rationally first, because that may not be smart.

Sara looked at me.

What is it sir? I asked.

He lowered his head.

Angel play the loop.

The hologram started and we saw Harold's familiar house. A high circle around, then a pause, then a zoom on a window bay in the north second story. One was glass. Mari and I glanced at each other.

That was unusual.

We saw a figure behind the glass. Then stepping to the glass.

The hologram froze with the window in full frame, the figure in full view.

A young woman in a white dress, long dark hair, one hand holding a necklace and the other a small red heart bracelet attached to the necklace. She held it pressed to the glass. She seemed to look right at the camera and smiled softly. She was radiant.

I caught my breath in my throat.

Mari and Sara gasped at the same time.

We had seen that smile so many times.

Dr. B got up slowly and went to her, touching the pendant, then her cheek.

It's Jessica he said.

My little girl Jess.

The Lost Heart
3

We stared in stunned silence.

Someone downstairs dropped something.

Mari and Sara put their arms around him. I was standing in front of Jessica. Staring at the heart bracelet, hoping standing closer would help me process this impossible girl in that impossible place. Hoping I could see some clue that would help us free her. I knew this would change everything but couldn't go there yet.

He turned to me and I touched his face as I touched hers.

Mari and I had been there in the beginning. A broken man carrying a black cylinder walking through a storm. We had seen him and six others coming towards us, slogging through mud, constantly looking back, huddling at the front door of our Church bunker. They had no home and no place to go with cannibals lurking. They were ill-prepared to defend themselves. I knew I had to let them in.

They helped Dr. B to his chair. I kept staring at Jessica.

Mari had peered from the basement door as I let them in, blade in hand. We gave them water and heated some soup on an open fire.. They slept shivering on the pews while Mari and I slept in the basement. Mari cried on my chest as they sobbed in anguish through the night.

At dawn we woke them. The man with the black cylinder we recognized right away. Richard Bohman. The Einstein of our generation. We knew the black cylinder was important. His friends were two colleagues from his lab; a doctor, nurse and janitor from the base hospital. A woman who had fallen in behind them. They had their clothes and little else. Fort Worth was on fire.

Mari was telling Dr. B we would get her out and he was saying hold on let's talk about it.

They had fled the lab and hospital as Hags stormed in. Most were killed or captured. The nurse had seen Dr. B's wife and baby taken. Annie and Jessica. Annie was a doctor, and famous as the wife of the famous man.

That day we had laid the foundation for our survival. The great man's sad monotone sparked a little when he talked about Stealth. He told us what he needed. We organized scrounging forays. We set down rules. We looked out for each other and stayed hidden while he worked to exhaustion in the basement.

Sir I said, what is the significance of the heart pendant?

When we brought Jess home from the hospital I gave Annie a heart pendant with a matching bracelet for Jess. They each had an identity transcriptor embedded. The lab was going to go Stealth and I wanted Annie and Jess to be able to see it if anything happened. I knew no self-respecting Hag would be caught dead with heart jewelry.

IDT had been ubiquitous among the population at one time, biological transcriptors in the blood stream that worked like an ID card. Computers in your blood. ID was one of the more mundane functions, as transcriptors could also monitor every function of the body. The IDT outside the body was different, however. This had been theoretical. The heart pendants were prototypes of what he called Portable Q. When perfected in the basement seventeen years ago he was able to cluster visual transcriptors in a matrix stabilized by a laser. Scalable Stealth was born. If you had the blood IDT or the PQ heart pendant or bracelet, Angel turned the Stealth off. We could see the Church inside a blue laser bubble.

There were several questions and I wasn't sure where to begin. I knew which one should be last.

Sir, you know Mari is right. We have to go get your girl. With my charm and Mari's body they have to let us in.

He laughed, wiping away a tear, breaking the tension.

But she looks happy he said. She's never known me. I'm sure she thinks Harold is her Father. Who else but his daughter would be treated that way? She looks happy and clean. Look at her. She would hate us for kidnapping her and dragging her across the Scald away from the only family she's ever known.

He had a point. I could not recall ever seeing anything clean in Hagtown, much less white. Maybe she had a reasonably good life hidden away in Harold's pain palace like the young Buddha. If you never see anything else you think this is just the way life is. You get a white dress and peasant thigh for dinner. Everyone outside the palace suffers and starves. This was hard to fathom knowing who her parents were. Did she know at some level she was in an evil place?

She was the daughter of a great physicist and great doctor - questioning things was in her DNA.

She does look happy Mari said. But maybe it's because she knows you're out here somewhere and coming to get her. She knew to stand in that window and press the heart to the glass. She knew to look up and smile. Somebody has told her.

Which drone was that? I asked.

A DJI Phantom he said. She wouldn't have been able to see it from that distance most likely. But at two hundred feet and down she would easily if it was moving. Hovering she would have to look right at it but a low levels they stand out. Not like the old days when jets and hovers filled the sky.

Our little drone fleet had a modified version of Stealth. When they flew out of the Church matrix they flew out of Angel's control, so they were outfitted with a fixed version of Stealth. The transcriptors on the hull were entangled with visual transcriptors top side and simply reflected the sky above. At speed they were a subtle smear streaking across the sky.

So it is possible she has seen poppers Mari said.

Poppers were drones self-destructing below one hundred fifty feet. We had lost a few over the years. High winds, freak storms, battery failure. We had discovered some C4 in a Texas Nazi bunker and fitted the drones. Below one fifty the detonator fired if outside the Stealth matrix. The explosion was downward for affect. Even a small amount was spectacular.

I once found a dying Hag in the Scald who fled after a popper went off. He said Harold told them poppers were God striking Rebel Angels swooping in to steal children. If a child disappeared, it was punishment from God and there must be penitence. The penitence was always a parent of the missing child going to the chopping block. It was his little boy who had disappeared.

We knew better what was happening with the children.

It's possible said Dr B, But not likely. Even if you were staring at the sky all day the chances of seeing one descend to detonation would be remote. Like a falling star. But that brings up another strange thing about this, and there are many. Why have we never seen her before?

That was a good question and none of us had an answer.

So who could have put her up to this? asked Sara.

Only one person, I think. His voice trailed off.

Sir, since Jessica was a new baby I think it means Annie had to survive I said. Harold would have known who she was. Everybody knew who she was. And didn't you say she wore an ID at the hospital? His soldiers would have known who she was.

He needed her alive. He would have a doctor in town and the wife of a famous man.

I chose not to continue with the thought she and Jess would be great bargaining chips.

But we haven't seen Annie either he said. All these years, visuals every day, and nothing.

True said Mari. But can you tell me what any woman in Hagtown looks like? They wear those stupid hats and veils and have to look at the ground around men. Most of the time the drones are following Harold and the boys around or watching some crazy shit at the chopping block. We hardly ever see the peasants except when they are pulled into Harold's orbit or are having something horrible done to them. And they all look the same in that filthy brown leather and those stupid long skirts.

My girl would have turned the Hag Patriarchy on it's nasty head. I thought about her walking up the Hagtown boulevard in yoga pants swinging her blade.

We have to assume Jessica lives with Harold but comes out dressed like all the other women. But we know where she lives. Annie is tougher since we don't have anything. But if we can get Jessica first she can lead us to her.

If she knows who she is I said. If she's the town doctor she will. But odds are Annie is sworn to keep the secret. Harold wouldn't have her regaling Jess with how great her Dad was...is...or teaching her the scientific method.

Everyone let that sink in for a minute.

Dr. B knew we would never sit here in our stealthy bank tube comfort while his daughter was in Hagtown. But he loved us as his children and I knew he was torn.

Sir, trust us. We can do this. I'm the greatest short blade samurai alive and the greatest long blade is standing next to you. We have the Mood suits and we know the Hags will run from Rebel Angels. We have the smartest pit crew of all time. And the best looking.

I'm not worried about your skills my boy. He took Mari's hand.

I'm worried about two against twelve thousand. And two thousand of them are some of the worst men who have ever walked this earth. And without you two I'm not sure the ten of us would survive. If your missing skills didn't kill us the heartbreak would.

Then there is only one option Mari said.

We both come back with Annie and Jess I said.

––––––––––––––

We called a meeting of the twelve and showed the hologram.

Their reaction was the same as ours.

We had decided to leave at midnight. We would walk two hours to the truck circle, take a thirty minute break, then two hours to the Mission on the hill overlooking Hagtown, arriving well before dawn.

We gave everybody tasks. Sara and James prepared our grub packs, twelve oatmeal bars and water canteens. Dr. B huddled with Jacob and Jeri, brother and sister physicists. We called them the J's. They were working on ways to use the drones to help the mission. Monique was the doctor and was checking our vitals with help from Michelle. Michelle was a young girl of about twelve who ran breathless into our Stealth bubble one day last year. The bad men chasing her ran right on by as Mari and I stood with blades drawn. Monique was her Mom now. Michelle shadowed her everywhere, watching and learning. Lawrence hadn't been feeling well so he had sentry duty all day in the chair. Adam and Hannah would handle the days meals and anything else that came up.

Mari and I spent the morning in the vestibule sharpening our blades. The Mood suits hung behind us, looking like chrome diving suits. We needed to do planning but thought some shut-eye was a good idea first. We lay on our mat for twenty minutes with the big-eye and gave up.

I started some coffee and went to the portholes.

I thought about the two against twelve thousand.

We were the Samurai of the Scald we were. Blades, hand-to-hand. The machete was part of our body, the knifes felt like our hands. Lethal. We trained in the Scald to adapt. Month after month, year after year, increasing stamina in small increments. I could jog with her on my back for a mile in fifty-degree C. We could both run two miles flat out. We were beyond any Special Ops ever deployed in many ways, with the exception of firearms.

We had decided in the first days no guns. There were plenty to be found scrounging around - it was Texas after all. Ammunition properly stored could last a long time. But with a population of twelve we had to beat the Hags with Stealth and our wits. Guns were anti-stealth. No matter how many guns we had we could only hold twenty-four in defense, and if discovered by a thousand hungry Hags it would be pissing in the wind. And guns made suicide easy. We all had nightmares. Eating a gun barrel would have been a relief some nights.

Guns with the Hags were a different story.

Dr. B said in the early years after 58 there was constant gunfire. As a boy, I remembered random gunfire was just part of life. Sometimes it was firefights with pockets of survivors trying to fend off zombies, sometimes bigger tribal battles. There were the big victory celebrations shooting at the stars all night. As the survivors began to congeal around the strongman Harold, one could trace over the years a fairly linear decline in gunfire, as ammo supplies presumably tightened, but also for a darker reason.

As a taste for human flesh grew from occasional field necessity to a staple, guns became the last resort for killing. Having his soldiers pick shot out of their teeth while they ate gunpowder flavored flesh was a fast way to get on the bad side of Harold. And his good side was bad. So, blades became the weapon de rigueur, and those who wielded a sharp one with skill proved valuable at the chopping block. A skilled executioner could keep a victim alive if body parts were lopped off in a certain sequence. Fingers, toes, and slabs of thigh were tossed in the crowd to be fought over like hyenas on a zebra.

One of the worst visuals any of us could remember was a filthy child crawling from underneath a hyena frenzy to gnaw on a finger.

Visuals once showed a lot of target practice in town. This had dwindled to Harold and Hoss taking two or three pistol shots in his backyard every month or so, another sign of low ammo. But we knew that at any time they could stumble across a right-but-it-didn't-matter doomsday prepper's buried shipping container packed with guns and ammo, and be in business with a million rounds. But this would run out fast, as the Hags were not known for conserving a bounty. God will provide more so fire away.

Mari and I knew this was a risk, but nothing we could do about it. The Mood suit was a highly ductile titanium-carbon alloy, incredibly skin-like but providing good protection from projectiles. We would have surprise and darkness on our side, and a reasonable assumption any guns had sand-laced mechanisms and lousy shots firing them in the dark. Cleanliness and discipline were not real big with Hags.

They valued rage and brute force, a bloody continuum that naturally terminates when you eat your enemies, for real. Hags were the flip side of the circle of life. Circle of death. You kill every living thing and make it sorry while dying it was ever born, eat it in celebration then shit it out the next day. Back to the dirt to start the cycle again. From star matter to shitty dirt and then start over. Their God was a big prankster but nobody got the joke.

Mari came up behind and wrapped her arms at my waist and laid her forehead between my shoulders. Grinding about Hags and their God always ended like this and made me gloomy.

Don't worry I said. I'm won't be gloomy. We can't afford it. This mission will require a good attitude and a lot of swagger.

A positive attitude is an essential element of any mission she said.

One of our mantras.

We both got swagger and I got the sway.

Hell yes you do.

And...we had to get back for Dr. B. It was fate of humanity level stuff. There were almost certainly bands of survivors holed up around the world, having made it through courage and luck. But I was pretty sure none had a Bohman and his Angel. He seemed to me the best hope for humanity. A building block. We were his guardians.

I put that out of mind for now.

Let's run visuals while we talk I said. Angel give us the last visual you have of the truck circle.

The halfway point and our only stop.

A hologram dated October 20 came alive. Twelve big pickups in a circle along the eastern edge of the desert, tires long gone, their once husky shoulders slouching with age. Most of the tall side pipes meant to look like the big rigs were still intact, although some leaning and some missing. Nobody knew how they got there. We guessed they were abandoned in the decade before the Water Wars, when climate chaos had the planet in turmoil. Another century they would be big lumps in the sand. In a millennia dust in the wind.

One of our favorite games at the supper table was to spin fantastical yarns to explain the mystery. I described a coal roller truck show where they rounded up to mimic a circle jerk to see who could pump out the biggest cloud of coal smoke from their revving diesels. The black toxic cloud overwhelmed everyone and they all died of smoke inhalation. The townspeople were so happy they left the trucks as a monument to their suddenly clear views of the road and breathable air.

Mari had laughed so hard she cried.

Niki, she said. I know there are snakes in there.

Don't worry love I'll protect you, in my best deadpan.

I know she said, never looking away from the trucks. I know.

Her phobia of snakes was deep. I really *did* have to protect her from snakes.

Nothing looked out of place with the trucks so I asked for the Mission on the hill. Our recon point before entry into Hagtown. A good view and secure through the power of belief - Hags wouldn't enter a Catholic church. They thought it was the home of Rebel Angels.

They were right about that.

Hitching Catholicism to the forces of Hell was no accident, as the root of Hagian belief was nurtured in the soil of Christian fundamentalism. The old-timey preachers had railed against the elaborate rituals and pointy hats as paganism. The Vatican was in league with the Illuminati to create one world government with the anti-christ as head, or something. This fringe element had been in the shadows in the twentieth century, but saw a Talibanic rise in the middle of this century as the social and economic orders began to break down. The nukes didn't finish us off. It was the weather and damned religions.

Weather chaos was deemed proof of God's wrath. The near dissolution of the Catholic church over rampant perversion among priests was also evidence of God being quite pissed. Finding out the Vatican had spied for China before the

Water Wars was the last straw for the faith in America, and the Hags spent several years purging Texas of Catholics by making examples of them on the chopping block. Their status was on par with Muslims.

The Mission on the hill was once a sublime example of an old west Mission. With a panoramic view to the west and south and a high bell tower, it was easy to imagine the call to Mass echoing far and wide. Like our humbler smaller Mission, it was built with thick adobe walls over a stone foundation and fortified with big timbers.

Mari and I had been inside once, ten years ago scrounging for supplies during a particularly lean year. We didn't linger with the proximity to Hagtown. I remember heavily shellacked dark wood pews and a plain crucifix on the back wall, in keeping with the plain and humble existence of the former congregation. Hundreds of years of pilgrims had worn a path in the stone floor to the altar, darker than the floor at the pew edges. Even with enough prayers to wear down stone it still ended up a hotel for demons. Go figure.

We were silent as the drone did a slow 360. As it panned across the front I lost focus, admiring the pastoral scene of the humble tan adobe against the blue sky white sand backdrop. Mari was on the job watching the door and windows and told Angel to go back.

The front entrance came into view and she said hold.

Niki It's been a long time, but I thought we closed those doors.

We did. Maybe the wind caught them.

Maybe. But check the window to the right. Angel continue please.

Angel hold the window and zoom. Now loop first appearance of the window for five seconds.

The window was tall rectangle. In the back of the sanctuary a shadow seemed to move. We watched the loop over and over.

Coyote's fear Hags but not Rebel Angels, I said. The stone floor would be a good cool place to lay.

Maybe she said.

Angel go to the Hagtown visual. Give us the perimeter then down the boulevard.

The perimeter fence was cyclone wire layered up to twenty feet high. Heads in various stages of decomposition were tangled in razor wire around the main north gate.

Peasant Town was Harold's first buffer, rimming the town perimeter with thousands crammed into shanties. Ragged roof tarps fluttered in the wind like blue and brown flags in a medieval fair. They crammed to the very edge of the huge town Square, traditionally in the center of town, but relocated here for expedience. Prisoners would be brought in the main gate into the square and taken to a maze of holding cells behind the altar and chopping block. Or just lined up and chopped without delay if everyone was hungry.

There was an unusual amount of activity going on. Tables and benches being set up around the edges of the Square, people milling to and fro. Big tin pitchers lined up waiting for hooch. There had been a couple of big explosions over the years and we figured it was the moonshiner getting careless after having sampled too much product.

Dia de Muertos I said. Begins tomorrow. Day of the Dead. Their biggest party of the year and a lucky break for us. Probably. Maybe. It could make things much easier or much more complicated.

The drone moved deeper into town.

Harold had put two elders in charge of Peasant Town.

Smilin' Pat was an original Harold loyalist and former Oklahoma evangelist who had formed a tribe after 58. They had roamed Southern Oklahoma and North Texas raping and pillaging. Pat has this big set of really white chompers and during the carnage would be smiling. He went a little too far south in Fort Worth in his last evangelical foray, and ran into Harold and his posse. After praying about it he decided to join rather than be eaten. Harold seemed to like him, as he was always laughing when he was around. That shit-eating grin must have been infectious. He had been an Aristo in the upper class, but got caught a few years back buggering one of Harold's young bodyguards and his punishment was exile to Peasant Town.

Lucky was lucky because he was possibly a former Muslim who was alive in Hagtown. He had blended in at first, but then best we could tell someone labeled him a Muslim. That was really bad luck, like being called a witch in Salem, but what happened next earned him his name. We watched on visual as he was dragged to the chopping block, where Harold seemed to be in a lively dialogue with the rabid crowd. It was impossible to read lips in Hagtown with all the filthy beards and dirt gazing, but the crowd seemed to object to eating a

Muslim - presumably on religious grounds. Harold ordered him released from the chopping block and he was handed a blade.

A duel to show my God is bigger than your God.

Instead Lucky placed the blade at the bridge of his nose and sliced it off. Harold was so impressed he made him Peasant Town co-elder, also presumably to the chagrin of Smilin' Pat the Baptist.

Only in Hagtown would a guy who chopped his own nose off be called Lucky.

The drone flew straight and true up the boulevard snaking out of the Square. The shanties were packed in tight right up to the Soldier Town boundary. Outhouses flowed into open latrines that didn't seem to have a direction to flow. Being a peasant meant you got to scrounge the wasteland of Texas all day, hoping for a shiny bauble to present to Smilin' Pat. On the way in you found some wood for the incessant drum fires and pits and for supper you fought for meat in the square to supplement the bugs you ate for lunch. You obeyed Harold's revised nine commandments or you went to the chopping block. He dropped the wife coveting thing after God spoke to him in a vision - possibly while in the throes of coveting - and thus it was.

The drone held steady and the shanties became actual houses.

Soldier town. Home to Harold's posse and their families. His old warlords and their sons and grandsons, all very armed and very savage. Loyal to the death to Harold. Answer only to him and the boys. These roughly two thousand men can move about town at will, but a woman must be with a man outside Soldier Town. Harold used the peasants as a human shield from any invasion, and his posse as a shield from the peasants. Run by his oldest warlord, an old Air Force Colonel named Hoss who was about five foot nothing and a buck forty and had once famously called for America to become a theocracy or perish. He got his wish, sorta.

We called him Hoss the Boss.

There were groups of soldiers hanging around front yards, looking like they got an early start on the festival.

With everybody drinking and screwing, said Mari, this might be easier than we think.

The guards and soldiers will definitely not be sharp I said. And if we use their clothes we could get past drunk guards.

The Mood suits would be shimmering bright red with dull chrome helmets on our heads. So, successful mingling would be directly related to the amount of hooch consumed.

The visual moved through Soldier Town into the biggest homes in town - other than Harold and the boys. Aristo Town. The tarped roofs were new and blue. There was no grass, but the dirt was more attractive. The Aristo's had bribed their way into favored status with Harold. They had been the Texas wealthy, land-owners or oil rich or grifty politicians, features often present in one individual. They bought status with gold and jewelry and daughters. We knew of two aging former United States Senators and several State mucketies. They were enjoying their twilight years with the base.

As the drone move up the boulevard the bustle of the pending festival gradually died out. Harold and the boys were the center of town, the black hole of the galaxy. Nobody wanted to test the event horizon and get sucked in.

I could hear Dr. B's red sandals clomping down the stairs.

Kids I forgot something he said. I'm embarrassed but in all the excitement…tomorrow is Jessica's birthday. Her eighteenth. Probably makes no difference but thought you should know. I don't know that she knows it's her birthday. Probably not.

I looked at Mari.

Thank you, sir. We will have her and Mom back in time for a birthday party Monday.

He smiled and hurried back upstairs.

He's very distracted I said. Understandable.

You think she knows it's her birthday?

Only if Annie told her. Or had someone tell her. Annie is sharp, so you know she is getting messages to her, even if not risking the big truth. But she probably got the birthday message to her a long time ago. The best chance we have is if Annie saw a drone and got Jess to the window. Otherwise…

Otherwise she's in a white dress inviting us to town on her eighteenth birthday on the first day of the Day of the Dead. And those just happen to be the two most important days for Hag girls to get married, or more accurately, auctioned off.

Yep. Not a trap at all.

Lions and Lambs

4

The twelve of us had supper a little later than usual. The mood was somber so I told jokes to lighten it up.

Why are some atoms Catholic?

Because they have mass.

Everybody rolled their eyes except Dr. B and the J's. They thought it was hilarious.

We had some perch and kale and potatoes. As we were finishing up everyone began wishing us well, and things got a little emotional. We had never tried anything this daring. Scrounges could be risky when dealing with strays or scouts and sometimes a posse. But walking into the belly of the beast...

We hugged and assured and went to our cubicle. I held her and we put our foreheads together and didn't say much. We knew what we had to do.

Near midnight we met Dr B in the vestibule and suited up.

The Mood suits had originally been called Chromes due to appearing as such, although not as shiny. They were like pulling on a second skin, much live a diving suit, covering everything except our neck and heads. Designing a bullet-proof titanium-carbon alloy into a suit this lightweight was incredible. Just as incredible was what happened when we pulled them on. Mari had been the first to try one and the dull chrome began to shimmer. Dr. B and I stood and watched in awe as the visual transcriptors in her suit entangled with her blood trancriptors, creating an oscillating shimmer between deep black and dark red. When calm we appeared mostly black. When excited red. It was hypnotic to watch.

The original design had the visual transcriptors capable of fixed Stealth outside the matrix. The oscillating shimmer at first seemed a terrible idea that had to have Stealth. Hags would see us coming from across the Scald. Then we realized a fundamental truth about our situation. We needed to be hidden away until we didn't. If we were seeking them out, we needed an edge. The Hags blamed Rebel Angels for all they couldn't explain. Demons causing mischief. They spent entire lives waiting for a miracle from their God that never came. But this - this was demons walking the earth and they were real, right here, right now. It would strike fear in their heart. It was a paradox we talked about a lot. The further technology advanced the deeper their faith in superstition. Create the illusion they desperately want, that was our edge. And if you prove the Devil, you prove the God. Their fear would become their joy.

And if anyone decided to take on the Devil, we had a long blade at our side and two short blades on our shoulders and we knew how to send them to hell.

Our helmets resembled a Roman Centurion galea without the plume. They were dull chrome with a slide down reaching to the lower throat, covering everything but the eyes and side of the neck. A flexible tail-piece protected the back of the neck. They were extremely lightweight, made of the same titanium-carbon alloy as the Moods. These had been prototypes molded without transcriptors. The only two in existence.

Supplies were in a low profile back pack. Canteen, oatmeal bars, Swiss Army knife and a pirate scope. The scope was retractable so we usually talked like pirates when they were pulled. They were military grade lenses and powerful.

We suited up and said goodbye to Dr. B and hit the Scald, shimmering red.

We walked at a brisk pace. We could see moonlight reflecting off the party barge far to the west - our name for a sunken boat from back when the Scald was a lake.

The trucks were on the eastern edge of the Scald at the base of the Sage. We called the climb out the Sage as it was pocked with sagebrush and creosote. It snaked along the edge of the Scald, a meander we would follow past the trucks to the Mission. We would recon from there tomorrow and go in at sundown.

Thirty minutes in I felt an urge to glance back at the Church. I thought about Lot's wife turning to a pillar of salt and that decided it. I turned towards Mari and she looked back with me. Our faint blue dome we called home. We watched for the laser, our breathing steady, the Moods pulsing deep red. The dome glowed along the laser line with a shimmering blue canopy trailing. As the laser line disappeared into the sand the shimmer slowly fell through the descending hues of blue, fading to pale. It was like watching a blue bubble breathe.

We turned without a word and set off again.

The moon was waning, big and bright. A distant chirp of a bat flight grew louder, then black-spotted our moon. Moving up into the Sage after a scorpion hunt. The blink of a larger shadow shot across the moon seconds later.

Did you see that? Mari asked.

I think so.

Maybe a hawk.

The cooling desert air felt good. I breathed deep. My burr tingled against the helmet. A breeze was coming down off the Sage, bringing a hint of sage and creosote. In the rare rainfall, the smell would blossom into a lush hot earthy you wanted to bathe in.

This was an easy hike for us and we made good time. We hadn't been to the Truck Circle in a couple months and Mari was thinking about it.

Why did guys drive those? They drank gas and belched smoke. I assume it was guys driving them.

Yeah, I said. Guys mostly. And I don't know. Young men displaying their plumage and all that I guess. Mom used to say the taller the truck the smaller the smuck.

I would have liked your Mom.

I would say you and she are a lot alike but that would be creepy so I won't.

Do you think they really impressed girls? I would have cut their tires.

I think the boys got them to ride but not the ride they wanted. And of course.

You're such a clever boy.

We walked silently for a stretch and the truck circle came into view. We paused to have a look. I pulled Mari's scope from her pack and she said "arrrrrrgh" as I pulled it open. I smiled as I focused in.

I found the trucks. I steadied the scope and took a long hard look.

Anything?

Pull my scope I said.

She pulled it and took a second to zero in.

We watched quietly.

Niki what the hell is going on?

I don't know. That doesn't make much sense. Let's have a closer look.

Are you sure?

When we get close fall in behind me. If I see any I'll tell you to put your hand on my shoulder. Close your eyes and we'll walk right on through. You know I won't let any near you.

Ok.

She fell back on my flank and moved closer as we closed in. Between the trucks dozens of yellow eyes were peering at us.

We reached the edge of the trucks where wild ponies were stamping and flicking tails and shaking their manes. But they didn't run. Mari put her hand on my shoulder. We walked between two beautiful ponies, one black and one white. They bristled and shimmered in the blue moonlight. The black one watched us with big dark eyes, shaking his head as if to say yes, go on in. I could have reached out and touched him. We kept moving towards the center as if in a dream. We were between two trucks and the yellow eyes emerged from wolves as we drew closer. I stopped at the front of the trucks.

What had to be fifty or sixty Gray Wolves were in the circle. Most sitting, some standing, all watching us. But not moving. A big one close to us pawed at the sand and tilted his head towards the moon, and began to howl. Heads rose across the circle as they all joined in. We were for a moment the last two on earth, man become Rebel Angel, evolving back full circle into the most primal.

Niki.

I know baby.

She was against my shoulder.

Wolves did not run in packs this size. This was several packs. Wolves did not behave this way, ever.

The leader just stood and watched us.

A sudden movement off my shoulder opposite Mari. A rat scurried from the inside a rusty rim and stopped. He sat there licking his front paws. A snake - big - slithered in behind him and curled up, his tail fencing in the rat. The rat lowered his front paws to rest on the snake's tail, never taking his eyes off us.

Close your eyes baby.

Her hand started to tremble.

I'm going to turn to my left and walk slowly back the way we came. Nothing is close so no worries. Just walk normal.

She said nothing and I turned and walked back between the ponies.

We kept moving a piece and I turned to hug her and see if we were being followed. She was shaking. It's ok I said. They aren't moving and we are clear. They are a long way off. Let's move on around and head up to the Sage on the other side. Stay on my outer shoulder.

Ok.

We kept our distance and moved up into the Sage a good distance south of the circle. I found a clear spot with a log and we took a rest. She was back to Mari now that the snakes were over there and we were over here. She sat against me just in case. We had some water and a carb bar. I kept looking through the scope at the circle. We weren't saying much.

What do you think?

I'm still not processing that scene she said. Predators and prey hanging out, unafraid of us. That howl. What the hell.

Their instincts are gone I said. That's not possible but we just saw it. They seemed to be...one. And we were welcome.

We went quiet for a minute, chewing.

It's like the lion lying down with the lamb she said, looking through the scope.

I know Revelation was trying to say enemies would get along in the end, but aren't lions and lambs going to hell with the the rest of us? So, what is the point.

I don't know she said. I asked a preacher once if my puppy would go to heaven with me and he said no. But my Mom said yes. So, there is some debate.

What an asshole.

The carb bars were chewy as hell and sticking to my teeth.

Heaven would suck without cats and dogs. You would think God and the Devil would work out some sort of arrangement regarding good boys and bad doggies. And tell us what it is.

I was trying to remember where my fingers had been so I could pick at my teeth. She was looking at the ponies.

They really are beautiful.

Did you look at the wolves or were your eyes closed?

I saw them. She nudged me with her elbow.

They are something special. i can't really describe how I felt when they howled.

I know. Of all the things we've seen in this crazy life this ranks right up there I said.

That it does my love. That it does.

I would kiss you but our mouths might stick together.

She kissed me anyway, laughing.

We stowed the scopes and canteens and headed south.

We felt good after the stop and were moving fast, Mari in front. The sage and creosote smell was strong, and the big moon was traveling with us. The two hours went by fast and we were near the ravine where we would climb to the Mission. Hagtown wasn't far on the other side of a big sandy hill that blocked the view south.

I liked being closer to the Sage more during the day than night. You might hear a few giant cicadas in the distance. I didn't know much about the central Texas cicada brood as a young man, but there were many varieties and the hum and buzz was very intense on hot summer days. One of them was called a Dog-Day and that was a good description of central Texas. Hot as hell. There wasn't a loud hum anymore but I had heard a few months back what sounded like a distant train whistle. A giant cicada. They had survived. Not as many but some.

That sound brought back childhood. I was born four years after the Water Wars and public schools were no more. Mother had taught me in the evening while I spent my days working to scratch out a living with Dad, learning how to take down abandoned oil rigs and iron fences to be turned into something we could sell. We would drag a haul back to our little cabin on the Trinity River.

Dad had been a soldier and taught me combat and survival skills. He was damaged from the wars, and his therapy was creating sculptures from the iron we scrapped. I would watch and hacksaw pieces that we would form with bailing wire into whatever vision we held. We would talk about this piece and that and spend hours just staring at it. Mom would watch from the porch in an old rocking chair, reading to Sis.

Our masterpiece was crafted from very old leaf springs pulled from a collapsing barn.

We cleaned them and shined them up - all but one.

With only three gently curving leafs we portrayed a tired soldier with shining wings.

What should we call it Niki boy?

Man as God I said.

It made him cry and I was upset but Mom said he was happy.

He fell sick one day and I went out scrounging for steel alone. Hags never came this way - nothing to loot and few to cook. But that day was different. They came across our cabin and killed Mom and Dad and Sister. They set our cabin on fire and cooked them on it. Man as God was all that was left.

I tracked the three down the river and when they laid down at night I killed them.

I was alone in a dark world.

Then came that night when the lambs were dying in Fort Worth.

Hear the crickets? Mari asked, her voice a smile.

We were starting up the ravine, up out of the desert to the plateau.

Isn't that beautiful?

It is my dear. It is.

Rebel Angels Versus Gabriel
5

The ravine was an old plateau washout carved by big rains of decades long past. We were up it quickly, using the roots jutting from each wall as pulls. It narrowed at the top and we slowed, careful to keep our helmets down.

The Mission stood two hundred meters across the flat, perched on the edge. A vast expanse of morning stars filled the big sky. Our moon traveler was low, touching the mission bell tower.

We sprawled out behind a low bramble patch at the edge of the ravine and Mari pulled my scope. The door that was cracked on the visual was still cracked.

I pulled her canteen out to take a sip, watching the door as she took a pull.

No movement inside. What you would expect for the middle of the night. We would go in soon.

Mari had the scope on the dark window and I was watching our six.

I thought about Jess. Our desert trek had given us time to chew on the preliminary theories.

If Harold has laid a trap I whispered, it will be too easy to find Jessica. But then things will get much harder. Probably at his house surrounded by the Hag Nation.

I'm hoping recon will help with that she said. What we know for sure is if he's behind it he knows about the drones.

So how did he find the drones? If Jess was seeing them and reporting it back to him he would think her touched in the head. If Annie had told him under...duress...it seems that would have happened years ago and he would already have used Jess as bait. And even if Harold had Annie's pendant there is still a lot of luck involved in seeing the drones.

So, let's say Harold doesn't know about the drones she said. What we are left with is a happy young girl trying on her wedding dress and holding her heart bracelet up for God to see and approve. We just happen to have a drone looking at her. Pure coincidence.

We will have to drag her out kicking and screaming I said.

Or, Annie put her up to it. Meaning Annie had seen a drone and knew it had to be Richard. And she's the only one who knew what the pendant was, so even if taken away seventeen years ago she would have looked for it ever since.

So, I said. Three scenarios. I think the least likely is Harold knowing. Pure coincidence has merit but the timing of it seems too much - her birthday, the festival. So, I'm betting on Annie knows we are coming.

She nudged my foot. I turned to see a big white cat running towards the front door. He slid through the crack.

That guarantees we have a human inside, I said. The cat wouldn't last an hour wandering out with coyotes about. The coyotes would only steer clear if a human is inside.

Could it be an escaped Hag? asked Mari.

Maybe. But fear of the Missions is strong. And it would have to be very recent or they would be starved. And any self-respecting Hag would eat the cat.

Another reason I loathe them she said.

So, let's assume the worst. We have an escaped Hag or Hags hiding in our recon position. The visuals haven't shown a posse lighting out so either an undiscovered recent defection or someone thought dead. Probably a single individual as more than one would have a posse on the prowl.

And scared witless. Now two Rebel Angels come strolling in the front door, she said.

And they run screaming out the back.

Let's circle around back to make sure we have a secure perimeter. You stay at the back door and go in on the count of ten as I go in the front.

We began circling right, crouched down. We moved towards the plateau edge until the back wall of the mission came into view. From the back wall to the edge of the plateau was fifteen meters. There was a sharp drop-off into a sandy incline plummeting two hundred meters down the sand hill to the Scald floor.

We walked straight to the far back corner, Mari's back to the wall next to the door. I stood next to her facing the opposite direction down the south wall. Now we could see our destination. Fires ringed Hagtown three clicks down. It was like a scene from Dante. We could smell the barrel fires that might have smelled of flesh. Might have been my imagination.

A faint scream arose from somewhere on the edge of town, dying in the desert air. The blanched white adobe walls reflected the fires, flickering like campfire shadows.

Now I said.

I moved quickly down the south wall.

I paused at the front corner to peek around.

I walked to the door and straight in with a quick side-step left, back against the closed door.

Mari's shimmer appeared one second later, back against the south wall to the left of the altar. She was five meters from the center pulpit, with thirty rows of pews between us. We stood silent, blades ready.

I sensed something in the dark corner to my right.

I slowly raised my long blade with a bent arm as a barrier between me and the corner, while reaching with my left to pull my right shoulder blade. I held it back ready to thrust.

Suddenly a scurry from the corner towards me - I took a quick step back ready to strike. In a split second the scurry was out the big door and gone.

The white cat.

Mari and I both were bright red.

I moved back against the door.

After five minutes, I began to move down the back wall to close the gap. If anyone was hiding among the pews it would provide an out through the front door. A Hag had no interest in taking on two Rebel Angels in a church. So, show them the door. They wouldn't go back to Hagtown to alert Harold, since defection meant the chopping block. Even if they did, their last words would be of Rebel Angels in the Mission. Yes, Harold would say to the crowd, we know that. Chop. Roars of laughter would be the last thing they heard.

I stopped an arm's length from Mari. Another scream rose and fell from the town.

Something on the far side of the altar. A creak? There was a single door leading down narrow wood steps to a small dank basement. We had been down there in our previous foray. Gave me the creeps. The unconscious of the church, under the altar in the ground, a place where a priest might do bad things out of sight of their God.

Creaking footsteps?

Mari began moving down the front of the altar towards the steps. We needed to be at the door when they emerged.

I moved parallel with her through the pews.

The stone floor was silent. Very clean and silent. Clean was a danger sign.

Mari positioned herself a blades length away. The door would open out and swing towards the wall. They would step straight into her blade arc, distracted by me dead center of their path.

A tall sliver of dusty blue moonlight fell through a window, across the door. We would get a good look at our creeper.

A creak right below the door, then silence.

Holding our breath.

The curved wood handle was carved in the shape of a robe. Or maybe an angel's wing.

Did it move?

It did. Slowly down.

Nary a sound from the other side.

Halfway down we heard a slow groan as the bolt pulled out. A pause.

Ten seconds went by, then twenty. Door didn't move.

At thirty seconds It began to open, almost imperceptibly. Creeper was looking for a small crack to check the front doors. Sightline would fall between Mari and I.

Heart thumping in my ears.

A tiny crack appeared. Minutes went by.

Suddenly it opened all the way and creeper stepped out, directly into the moonbeam.

He saw me and froze in terror with a loud sucking gasp.

In the dim blue light, I could see his frayed and dusty cassock. His clerical collar was dirty and sad.

Don't move priest, I growled. Are you alone?

He was gaunt and frail. Eyes as big as saucers, he hadn't breathed since the gasp.

He sensed Mari in is periphery and jerked back against the open door. I put the tip of my blade to his throat.

Answer the question priest. Are you alone.

Mari tilted her head to peek around the corner down the dark steps, blade resting on her outer thigh.

I never believed Rebel Angels existed he whispered, eyes clenched shut.

Well we do. Now answer me. That sad collar will look very funny without a head on it.

I'm alone. I give you my word.

Clasp both hands on top your head.

He raised shaking hands and clasped them over his thin black hair. He opened his eyes, looking at the floor.

Step away from the door.

He took a shaky step away, then another. My blade stayed on his throat.

Mari pulled the door shut. She pulled a wooden chair from the wall and wedged it under the angel wing.

We led him to a pew on the Hagtown side. We chose one with a good view of town from the window, close to the back of the sanctuary, and sat him down on the end.

Keep your hands on your head I said.

Mari took off her helmet and positioned on the front edge of the window to get a scope on town. I stood toe to her foot, facing the big doors, watching the priest.

Do you have water and food? I asked. I pulled off my helmet.

I need to go out for water. There is a well just over in the brush. I have some food in the basement, but not much.

We aren't after your water or food priest. Here.

I sheathed my short blade and handed him my canteen.

He took a long pull and handed it back, wiping his mouth with the back of his hand.

Keep your hands on the pew in front of you.

Dawn was peaking in.

I pulled a chewy bar from Mari's pack as she looked for Harold's place. I put it in her mouth and she took a big bite. I tossed him the rest.

He swallowed it without chewing.

Thank you. You must be human he said. Rebel Angels do not need food or water. Or blades. They would not be kind.

How would you know?

I guess I wouldn't. His eyes stayed down.

I'm curious as hell to know what a priest is doing in the basement of a mission next door to Hagtown in the year of your lord 2099.

The Hags won't come in here he said. But I suspect you know that already.

How long have you been here?

Six years, six months and five days.

Well tomorrow should be interesting.

He said nothing. His hands whitened as he gripped the pew.

Do you look after the white cat?

Yes. Gabriel.

Where is his food and water?

In the front corner over there. I was coming out to take care of him.

We will see to that in a bit.

The soft dawn light revealed some details. A face drawn by starvation. Eyes bulging and stained teeth too big for his skull. His black shirt was dusty but could have been worse. Darns held it together. His black hair was thin, more scalp than hair. A long neck that seemed insufficient to hold up his head. Clean hands but bony and spider-like. Surprisingly free of odor. He looked up at me. He was giving a cat food he could eat.

I felt pity.

We mean you no harm priest, as long as you do as we say. You will have food and water as long as you sit there quietly. So will Gabriel. If you wish to test us you will meet your lord on this day. Do you understand?

He shook his head yes.

Mari nudged me with her foot. Harold's place she said. She handed me the scope and I focused in. Harold's big double doors with matching crosses adorning each. He should be emerging soon to survey his kingdom.

Nobody in the glass window. I moved the scope up and down the boulevard looking for a white dress.

There were scroungers shuffling up the boulevard single file out of Peasant Town, crossing to the edge of Aristo Town where a narrow concrete road ran east to the perimeter. They would bring whatever they could find of value in a day's rummaging back at sundown. They also were made to bring wood, with haulers at the gate loading up their carts and making the rounds to replenish the pits. It was an all-day scrounging worm, every day. At dark when the gates were closing we would politely let ourselves in. The scrounger road met the boulevard only about one hundred meters from Harold's front door.

Our red shimmers were mixed with black. The priest was peeking up, slack-jawed.

Hagtown smoke was drifting out into the Scald. I imagined the smell in the Mission depended on the wind. A southern breeze brought smoke and flesh, all others the pleasant creosote and sage.

I handed the scope back to Mari and pulled a chewy bar from my pack and bit off half. Mari opened her mouth for the other half.

Go feed Gabriel I said to the Priest.

He rose with effort, still shaky. I knew he wouldn't try to run but I followed him to the front door. His backbone was visible through the faded black shirt, shoulders hunched. He pulled something from a cassock pocket and placed it in a small saucer. There was a wooden bowl of water next to it.

I stepped closer to see what it was. A giant cicada.

Gabriel may not come back while you're here he said.

We'll be quiet.

I took him back to the pew as Mari settled in for a long watch.

I handed him the canteen. When finished I tossed him a full chewy bar. I wasn't sure his teeth could handle them.

I put my toe back on her foot and relaxed a little against the adobe wall. We had planned to sleep but with the priest it complicated things. We would probably have to lock him in the basement for a couple of hours before we set out.

Mari nudged my toe. He's coming out she whispered.

I told the priest to lie face down on the pew. I sat my canteen on his back and told him don't move.

I positioned behind her with a scope and found the door.

First out was Franklin. His tooth chain was jangling and he had a dust cloud like a cartoon character as a trailing sycophant slapped his back. His greasy smile hinted at the oleaginous reek that was the rest of him. His hair was long and matted in typical Hag fashion. He had a blade slung to his waist at his left hand with shoulder blades peaking up beside his ratty locks. On his right hung a small sledge, flat on one end and dull-pointed on the other in what counted for high-tech among cretins. His getup was the fashionable mashup of leather sheaths and desert camo. Spaghetti Western meets American military on Fury Road.

A round leather drifter style hat with a draw strap was hanging down his back, topping a long leather tail hanging to his ankles. This was the battle strap. A metal cup was stitched in with a head loop cut out near the bottom. Adorning the strap were metal studs shaped into a big crucifix, designed to slow blades and bullets and scare off Rebel Angels. When they ventured out of town the strap was pulled between the legs and looped over the head, the cup protecting God's little spear. It was a sight to watch a Hag posse on one knee in prayer with leather tails splayed behind, all rising at amen to tuck and loop the battle strap over their heads. The biblical act of girding your loins. We called it tucking their tails.

Franklin's gait was all arms and legs. He was a big man, maybe six five two fifty.   The tooth chain framed his crucifix, green with a bloody Jesus. If you ever wondered what kind of idiot would put bloody Jesus on a green cross there he was.

The priest was mumbling a prayer into the pew.

All Hag soldiers had the crucifix around their neck, custom made as they wanted. It was a brilliant stroke by Harold. Kept them welded to the core faith while feeling they had a personal Jesus. Aristo's wore a white version of Harold's design - a clean Jesus - while peasants were allowed leather engravings or studs but no chains or jewelry. Impediment to slave labor I suppose. In a symbolic faux pas, with battle straps down the stud cross hung upside down and looked like it was being shat out into the head hole.

Next out was Levi. He was my size, not as big as Franklin, and was a better-looking specimen than Franklin. His hair was long but looked clean, as did the rest of him. His eyes were piercing, staring at Franklin as he moved down the dirt walk.

We had never seen Levi chop anyone. He didn't come out much.

He looked serious, even angry. Franklin was at the street lighting a cigarette in a drum fire. He was staring at Levi with a smug look. Levi stopped at the curb and folded his arms, Looking up towards our plateau. Franklin turned to watch the door, pulling a drag. A group of soldiers had assembled in the middle of the street, waiting on Harold.

We saw Harold's massive bulk and then the top of his head as he stepped out of the shadow. As he straightened up we tilted our scopes in unison to keep him in frame. Even in his mid-sixties he was an awesome site. His forearms looked like a normal man's leg. His upper arms were sheathed in straining leather. His long hair fell onto massive shoulders, framing a square jaw hanging from high cheekbones. His eyes were nordic blue with bushy eyebrows.

He paused on the stoop.

Ugly son-of-a-bitch said Mari

The priest started a new prayer for her soul.

I pulled back to check the room. Movement at the door caught my eye.

Gabriel sauntering in for his cicada. He wasn't afraid of no Rebel Angels.

The priest had sharpened senses from his monastic life. He stopped his prayer. Gabriel paused and stared at me with big green eyes, then ambled to his big green breakfast. The priest went back to praying into the pew.

I scoped back on the stoop. Harold was walking towards the street, looking at Levi. His eyes looked strange. His gold jewel encrusted cross hung from a chain that could pull a horse from the mud. His tooth necklace was bigger than everyone else's. His leather tail hung a little lower. The right hammer looked like a full sledge. His big blade was massive and dark. No shoulder blades, but a big hunting knife holstered on his giant leather chapped thigh.

Someone inside shut the doors.

We didn't know where Harold's harem stayed in the house. There were many bedrooms, and they probably shared rooms. But Jessica was different. She might have her own room, maybe top floor. We had decided if no visual we would enter where we last saw her.

Harold and his entourage moved down the boulevard to tend to his flock. A couple of blocks ahead you could see people shuffling toward the boulevard to see the King. I knew you could hear the teeth chains chattering as the big men walked. Harold drifted to the curb to pick up a little blond-hair girl, holding her high in his massive hands, then kissing her head and handing her to parents with four arms extended.

Why don't you get some shuteye I said without looking away from Harold. Couple hours.

No more than a couple hours she said, folding the scope.

She took the canteen off the priest.

We need you to return to the basement for a little while. If you need water knock on the door. We will let you out in a few hours.

He sat up.

I understand. But you should know I won't betray you. I have no way even if I wished to. And I've prayed. God approves of your mission.

I looked away from Harold towards the priest.

I doubt your God knows anything about our mission she said.

He paused and looked down at his hands in his lap.

You seek the Mother.

And the daughter in the white dress.

Peasant and Priest
6

Mari's blade was at his throat in a flash.

Gabriel scurried out the door.

Just when we were starting to like you she said.

You better enthrall us with how you know that, I said.

He was trembling again, eyes on the blade.

She came to me. Six days ago. She saw my scope reflect and she escaped and came here.

Who? asked Mari.

The Mother. She walked right in the front door without fear. I was praying on the altar and she walked right up to me.

What did she look like?

She was small. Dark hair. She had on a peasant long dress. I knew right off she was not a true Hag though.

How did you know that?

She walked right in. And she had a kind face.

Mari lowered her blade.

And?

She said she saw the sunlight on my scope. She knew I wasn't a Rebel Angel, and she had to give me a message.

He paused.

She said her husband was a great man, and if he was alive he would come for her and her daughter. She asked if I had ever seen him, or anyone other than a Hag. I told her no, but I had seen something that might give her hope.

What?

We used the same window you are using. I gave her my scope and told her to watch above the town. I tilted the scope up and she watched. She saw one. She asked me what it was. A drone I said. They've been there since I've been here. She started crying.

From this high angle, the drones became visible.

Mari sat down next to him, looking at me. She took a pull from her canteen and handed it to him.

Thank you for helping her, she said. Her name is Annie. Please tell us everything. Everything she told you.

She told me he was alive and watching. But she was among the peasants and wore a hat. He would never see her. And he would never see Jessica. Her daughter.

Why not Jessica?

She said Harold told her when they had captured her and her baby would survive under one condition. She had to be the town Healer. Harold saved her for this purpose, and God worked through her to heal the townspeople. And to never speak to Jessica again, or reveal the truth.

He paused and squeezed his eyes shut, mumbling a prayer under his breath. We waited, looking at each other, recalibrating.

Father, why have we not seen Jessica?

He looked at her.

Harold kept his word. The girl was leverage to keep Annie working, and leverage if her father was ever a threat. She was raised by his harem. The harem lives underground most of the time.

Underground?

Yes. She said Harold and the boys have basements, and they had spent years digging tunnels. The harem lives beneath his house most of the time.

How did she know this?

She is the Healer. She treated the harem but I don't think she wished to tell me why. But she said they lived better than most in town.

Did she describe the tunnels?

Harold's house is connected to Franklin and Levi. There is another running beside the cement road to the East gate. It connects with Harold's and opens up outside of town. There is also one leading to the altar in the town square.

Did she say if guards are stationed in the tunnels?

Yes, but only at the intersection where the cement road meets the boulevard. The three tunnels meet there. The only other guard is the entrance to Harold's basement. But two are stationed at the intersection. Only one when there is a sacrifice. The other waits under the altar for the best, umm, parts...to be handed down and carried off to Harold's house.

How did Annie get back into town?

She showed up at dusk. Her only purpose was to find out who was in the mission and give them the message then sneak back in. She stayed longer when she saw the drone, but not much. She would be missed and a posse would set out so she had to hurry. She had so much hope in her eyes. She became a different person. I hope Harold doesn't notice that.

He would become suspicious?

Yes. He is truly evil. I have watched the town every day all these years, and seen indescribable works of Satan. Newborn children taken from Mothers. Drunken soldiers doing unspeakable things. The peasants wear hats because of the sun, but they keep their heads down around Harold always. If he sees happiness he will take it away. Except during his sermons where you better act happy. I once saw him drag an old man to the altar after a sermon and gouge out one of his eyes, and...eat it.

Horrors we had witnessed as well.

He bowed his head to say a mumbly prayer.

Mari led me to the window while he prayed.

Can we be this lucky? she whispered.

Yes, I said. Dr. B said Harold would have met his match with Annie. Once she saw the drone she made a plan. She would put Jessica on display, hands on pendant, looking at the sky. She would give the priest all the details she could so we would have a chance. It makes sense.

She nodded.

Look at the intersection. That little shed we thought was just a checkpoint. That has to be the tunnel entrance. The chopping block I can't tell for sure but a trap door would be a good guess. It would have to be directly over the tunnel to pass ..... meat. Down.

I was imagining a flesh tunnel dripping with blood.

Could this be as simple as walking in through the East tunnel, killing three guards, taking Jessica and leaving the same way?

Possible but there's Annie. And now I think we need her first.

She could lead us to Jess.

———————————

Priest, how did you know about the white dress? I asked. Mari lightly touched his shoulder. He recoiled from her touch.

I'm sorry I flinch when you touch me he said. When she...Annie...left, she hugged me and I collapsed in tears. It felt like God flowing through me.

He lowered his head and sniffed a little.

She told me to watch for a new glass window in Harold's house. She said when it appears Jessica will appear the same day and I will know it's her. When I saw her in white...it was a vision.

He looked at me, waiting for a reaction.

Go on I said.

A vision in white. A sign from God. She was so clean.

We knew Annie had to have a friend in Harold's house.

So, Jessica normally doesn't wear white?

No, I don't think so. At least it didn't look like something that had been worn much, being clean and all. You never see white in town, even weddings and such.

Mari pulled out a chewy bar and took a bite, giving him the rest.

He chewed, thinking. A gentle breeze wafted through the pews. I smelled sage.

She said you would be watching Harold's house. You would see her, then you would come here. She said you might appear strange. Maybe other-worldly. But when I came out of the basement...I've never seen anything like you. I don't understand how you make this happen. He was looking at Mari's hypnotic red legs.

I started to say something, but she gave me the slow eye close and subtle no nod.

Did she give you a way to signal we had arrived? I asked.

No but she has a way for you to signal if you go to the East gate. She is stationed there every evening at dusk to tend to any injuries the gatherers have sustained. She said get her attention and she will come to you.

She is there every day?

Yes. They go out every day. She's there when they return to help them. She's a kind person.

Thank you for your help Mari said.

I will go to the basement so you can sleep he said.

You can stay here I said. Mari looked at me.

Thank you. But I have a bed downstairs and I will lay down for a bit also if that's ok. I will leave the door open. I hope I can see you off later.

Of course, said Mari.

We watched him disappear down the stairs.

We have to come back later and get him to the Church she said. He's a decent man but he won't last much longer here. And Gabriel.

Get the priest to the Church made me smile a little.

Of course. Although catching Gabriel may make fighting Hags seem easy.

We have a real chance now she said. Annie has given us a real chance.

Yes. The key is finding Jessica fast and getting out faster. Without being seen. Not easy.

Why not have Annie go find Jess and bring her to the East gate?

She is forbidden to speak with her. So the friend would have to escape with us or face the chopping block. That makes five of us trying to get across the Scald before Harold catches on. All assuming Jess and friend can get past Harold and the guards. There is also the complication of the Festival. That could hurt or hinder, we don't know. We've assumed everyone would be drunk and screwing so easy access - but it could also mean Harold keeps his harem hidden away from drunk soldiers. Or maybe they are part of the festivities, who knows.

Hopefully Annie. We can't be wandering around Hagtown asking where the women are.

We use the tunnels. The problem with tunnels is nowhere to hide. Besides the trapped like a rat thing.

Annie will have a plan she said. We don't know enough yet.

I thought about the slap on Franklin's back and Levi looking angry.

Franklin seems to have Harold's favor. I wonder what that was all about?

I think his favor has to be from being the eldest. It's a big deal in their Old Testament world. But you gotta figure Harold is weary of chopping parents up to cover for Franklin's evil. Unless Harold is part of it. Hell, Franklin may be his talent scout.

Could be I said. Wouldn't surprise anyone. But what we know for now is Franklin is happy and Levi is unhappy about some decision that Harold made on the eve of the biggest celebration of the year. So, it would seem to be more important than who gets a new window in their house. And Harold must not be too pissed at Franklin.

If he thought it was following God's law he might set aside his opinion. Would have to be something big. Successor. Choice of brides.

And there it was.

I knelt in front of her. Voices carried on the clean stone.

We can't let the white dress fuck us up here. She did look like a young bride in love. But that would mean Harold used her to draw us here and this priest is in on it and lying about Annie. But a lot of problems with that theory. For starters, why did he wait eighteen years to display her? He could have stood in the window himself rocking her as a baby. And it means Harold is in league with a reviled priest in a grand scheme to draw us to Hagtown. And the priest is living in a hole eating cicadas, so not exactly getting a good deal. And even though lying is an art form in the church, he seemed to be truthful. We scared the shit out of him and I think he spilled the beans. And if this was a master-stroke by Harold to draw us in, we would be surrounded right now.

But he doesn't want us except for supper. He wants Dr. B. So, he baits us into leading him back to the Church. Which mean if this whole rescue seems like a cakewalk we should be worried. And Harold has never had a clue where Dr. B might be - but if we head out north it narrows things down a lot.

We will know if a posse is following us.

True. But both heart pendants are down there. Jessica has one. If they know what direction we are heading they would eventually stumble onto us. And I'm betting Harold has Annie's pendant in his pocket.

We need to ask the priest if he remembers it on Annie. Since peasants aren't allowed jewelry she probably didn't. But maybe she stashed it. If we don't find the damn thing and they see what direction we leave we'll never get another good night's sleep.

How would Harold know it reveals the Church? Jessica only knows if Annie told her friend. I can't think of any reason she would do that. And I can't think of any scenario where Harold would know that. But your right - without it we'll never relax.

I think we have to assume the priest is telling the truth she said. If Harold knew the heart bracelet revealed the Church he would just send out a Scout wearing it.

Let's get some sleep I said. After some shuteye, we can ask the priest a couple more questions then get this show on the road.

I kissed her hand and pulled off my backpack for a lumpy pillow. While she settled in on the hard pew I stepped to the window to look for Jess or Annie. Found Harold straight away. Not that difficult to find the giant asshole. He was holding court in the Square, hundreds of peasants with heads down. The Square looked ready for the Festival. A typical drab Hagian scene, without color or joy. The joy was supposed to be in your heart or something. The whole town was mud brown. The people were just variations on this shade.

I spent the next couple of hours watching Harold and his entourage meander about. Mari had fallen asleep quickly. Like any good soldier you slept when you could. I had another chewy bar and sipped some water. She was slightly curled against the back of the pew, seeking its cold comfort in my absence. Her lithe titanium figure looked good. Go to hell for that thought. Oh well.

About three hours on I sat on the pew edge lightly touching her with my back. After a few minutes, she stirred and placed her hand on my back. She sat up and as she kissed my cheek I saw the priest at the stair door, watching. He looked down.

It will be ok she said as I lay down on the warm pew. I closed my eyes and drifted off.

———————————

I woke with a start, hand on my blade, a hand on my cheek.

It's me baby. Let's get this show on the road. She had that look.

Where's the priest?

I sent him down for the scope. Want to make sure he can actually see Harold's window from here.

You are reading my mind again dear.

She kissed my forehead and I got up, shaking my head awake. My cool black started to red up.

The priest creaked up the stairs and emerged with an old scope. She asked him to find Harold's window. He hesitated a second then expanded it out and leaned a little out the slim window. He didn't have to move it much and then it was still. He didn't say anything but held it still and pulled his head back.

Not a bad view she said.

She tilted it up looking for Harold's drone. After some back and forth she found it.

She folded the scope sharply and handed it back to him.

Thank you.

Priest I am curious about a couple other things, I said.

Do you know how long Annie has been stationed at the East gate?

A few months he said. She works during the day from a shack at the peasant boundary to the soldiers, right on the boulevard.

Can you show us?

Yes. He pulled the scope back apart and looked. He handed it to Mari.

It is last one on the left side.

So, a steady stream of people in and out?

Yes, I would say so. Soldiers sometimes but mostly gatherers.

Why do you think Harold has her at the gate every day now? Couldn't they just go to her shack?

Perhaps a gesture towards the peasants, I'm not sure. I know that doesn't seem like Harold but he seems to sense when to give a little.

One more question. Do you remember Annie having a necklace with a pendant?

He thought for a moment.

No, I don't think so. It could have been under her shirt maybe - but when she was looking through the scope I don't recall a necklace on the back of her neck.

I handed him a full chewy bar.

Thank you. We are heading out now. I want you to know once the mission is completed we will come back for you. You and Gabriel. You will have water, food, companionship, safety. You would leave this world among friends.

Mari put her hand on his shoulder. His eyes were welling up.

Thank you, my son. I know you mean that and you both are good people. But I must stay here. It is my penitence. It is God's will.

He bowed his head and I just stared for a moment.

I understand I said, even though I didn't. Mari touched his cheek and he leaned into it, putting his hand on hers.

It was a bright day, very calm. As we approached the sage brush line we saw Gabriel perched on the partially hidden well. The old adobe well was low and worn, jutting just above the brush. He had a scrawny shade tree whose shade was slim, but enough for a rangy cat. He had that statuesque cat pose going as he watched us cross the plateau watching him. He wasn't impressed.

We would vector back east then circle back towards the gate looking for a good spot to get within earshot of Annie. The gatherers had been forced further and further east as they stripped away the countryside. To offset the lowered production Harold had enlisted more gatherers. They came back with overlooked stashes of everything imaginable. The pillaging had been in blitzkrieg style; Harold's gatherers were the detailers who picked through the aftermath.

You did not come back empty handed.

The descent was fairly rapid as we meandered through the sandy sage spotted with scrawny trees. We were out of view from the town except for the eastern perimeter. The road was concrete to the perimeter gate, then a dirt path that looked as hard as concrete winding like a brown river off to the southeast. We wouldn't see anyone returning until just before dark.

If we could reach Annie before anyone returned that would be good.

I felt good after the sleep. Mari had a bounce in her step.

You are worried this is a setup she said.

The jury is still out on that.

Harold may have moved her out to the gate to tempt her into going to the mission she said.

That was my thinking. But something else caught my attention. He said Annie walked right up to him like coming in the mission was nothing. But she would have not known about the priest. She would have assumed it was rescuers when she saw the scope reflection. You would think there would be hesitation or disappointment or something. But maybe she knew what to expect because Harold made her come up here. Or maybe she never came at all and the priest is lying.

Either way a trap.

The meander down and back didn't take long. We were crouched behind a stand of sage looking at a shack just outside the Eastern gate. Like the rest of town, it looked terrible. Through a door in the middle we could see a table and chair with some shelves on the back wall. Nobody home.

We probably had all day to wait on Annie. I was wondering if the priest was signaling town right about now. I was able to get a scope on part of the boulevard while Mari kept an eye up the dirt path. We sipped water and ate and waited. We had shade but it was hot. The afternoon sun started dropping. I wondered if the gatherers would try to come back early to get started on the drinking. I was getting stiff and raised up a little to stretch my back.

Then things got interesting.

Space Cowboys Don't Need Boots
7

Battle horns wailed from the center of town. To soldiers this meant "get your ass over here now". There was distant shouting, then quiet again. It was that vibrating quiet with a low hum, when you could feel something was up.

What do you think?

Can't be good.

No sign of Annie, and the roads in both directions were empty. I couldn't decide if the battle horn would keep peasants away or bring them home. Probably the first. Whatever happened Harold would be looking for someone to pay. If you weren't in town better chance of surviving whatever it was.

Suddenly as if rising from the earth a very big Hag appeared on a dirt berm behind the shack.

He was about a hundred meters back off the road. He was looking for someone or something. Two more joined him on either side, one mumbling prayers and the other with a giggle tic. We pushed a little lower into the sand.

We found the tunnel entrance I whispered.

Bring her out! the big one boomed.

A gangly warrior with hair falling over his face appeared, dragging a woman by the hair. She had both hands on his wrist trying to ease the pain. She was bloody and beaten and half naked. He kicked her in the chest and she rolled backward down the berm into a dust pile. She tried to raise her head but had lost her air. She curled up so her body could find it.

Show yourself Rebel Angel! bellowed the big one. Show yourself now, or she dies.

He looked side-to-side to make sure they all were impressed.

Stay here I said.

Niki…

Trust me.

I rose up like the big Hag did, as if from the sand.

They all took a step back but the big one.

Jesus be our shield! prayer boy cried out in a trembly voice, shield trailing off with his courage.

I walked across the hard dirt road past the shack straight to her, the shimmer going darker as I walked through shadows of the big fence. I looked straight at the big one and pulled my long blade.

Now he took a step back.

She raised her head to see. Her face was a bloody mess, one eye purple and swollen shut. But I knew who she was.

I was in that battle zone where any sudden movement meant sudden death from steel. Staring at the big one. You could almost see the smell cloud rolling down the berm. My nostrils flared and tasted buds soured.

This will be your last day of beating women I said. Your God can't save you from me. Now let's get you started paying for this sin.

We will be judged by almighty Jehovah, not by a filthy spawn of hell growled the big one.

He reached for his blade. Hairy face dropped out of sight. He was back in the tunnel and that was not good. Prayer boy was fumbling for his battle horn. I right hand whipped my left shoulder blade and sunk it in his throat. He blew a feeble death gasp into the horn and fell backward as I whipped my right blade towards the giggler. It lodged in his mouth in a squealing burst of blood and teeth. He dropped to his knees, eyes crossed on the blade, the giggle tic now a gurgle tic.

I started to yell for Mari but she flew by my left towards the tunnel door.

The smart thing the big man could do now would be run down the backside of the berm blowing his horn. But being a Hag his blood was boiling with fear and rage so he came full on down the hill, a load of blubbafied muscle with blade swinging overhead. He was going to hack me into Rebel Angel paste.

Jesus kill this spawn of hell! Give me God strength!

I moved right to get him away from Annie. His hurtling bulk was gaining momentum. His fanged rotten teeth were bared with spittle dripping from his tangled red chin beard. His battle strap was up and festooned with a big be-jeweled cross that might have been gold. Someone of rank. Someone who was rank. The fetid wave enveloped me as he barreled in, a prayer growl gurgling from his ponderous gut.

I stood my ground.

At full speed and closing fast he raised for the kill strike, angling downward across my face. As the blade descended I stepped in and turned towards him, blade still down. Nothing he could do now but finish the strike on air, the heavy blade pulling him over as he fought to slow momentum, all happening in the blink of an eye. With a grunt, he tumbled shoulder down and over and barrel rolled like a hairy dough pin, all groans and clanging sounds. The wreck ended with him face down, not moving, arms at his side like he was peeing. Blood pooling around his groin. I got a foot under his shoulder and with effort rolled him over. His blade had pierced the metal loin cup and done a lot of man damage. I put him out of his misery and turned back up the berm.

Annie had her cheek in the dirt watching.

The giggler was on his side with one hand covering his ear and the other on the knife handle, pinwheeling, trying to pull it out. Blood bubbled over handle and hand, covering his forearm and draining into the dirt. I stepped on his head to stop the pinwheel then kicked the knife to end his life.

Annie was still watching me from her one good eye.

I'll be right back I said.

The door was a rusty steel tornado door laid open in a patch of thick sage, exposing the dark hole of the tunnel. I hunched and entered, listening. Silence. I dropped in the dark and saw a candle in the distance, maybe a hundred paces. There were railroad timber supports overhead held up by the same. I had to tilt my neck a little to walk. Walking a few paces then running. I stopped in the dark at the hundred-pace mark. Another candle in the distance, with pitch black in between. Then a red shimmer in the pitch. I ran to her.

It's ok he's down.

She touched my arm as my eyes adjusted.

I was listening she whispered. He never got to his horn but he yelled. I'm hoping these mopes are the tunnel guards.

We have to get back to Annie. We can seal the door I whispered.

I knew it was her she said.

We ran out of the tunnel. I shut the big door while Mari tended to Annie. I pulled prayer boy and the giggler to the door and slung them over it criss-cross. I pulled my short blades and wiped them on their battle straps.

Mari was cradling her, giving her water.

Annie, how long before the peasants come back I said.

They won't for now she whispered. They heard the horn and will stay away. There will be three blasts for all clear.

She took a sip as Mari dabbed at her eye with water.

Can you walk? Mari asked.

I think so. One of those bastards kicked my knee sideways so it may be torn. But I can limp.

We need to get you out of sight I said.

I can make it to the Mission she said. I can crawl if I have to. The priest will help me. You have to find Jess. Please. I know that's why you are here. They argued in the tunnel and made the big one call you out. You weren't supposed to be here until tomorrow but they believe Rebel Angels are full of tricks.

We're here for you as well.

I picked her up and we hustled across the dirt road to our sage cover.

What is going on Annie? Why would they do this to you? How would they know we were coming?

Jess is missing she said.

Mari was checking her knee and looked at me.

Missing? Where could she go?

Tomorrow is her birthday. She's ... eighteen. She closed her good eye tight and a tear ran from the corner. Mari pulled her face to her and stroked her hair.

Annie, listen. We will get her out. Give me some ideas on where she could be. Could she get out through this tunnel? Where could she hide? We have to hurry. If they are expecting us we have to find her. Now.

She turned to spit blood in the sand. Mari pulled her hair back, exposing scars on her neck and upper shoulders.

I was in Harold's house a little while ago. He summoned me. I go through the tunnels so the people don't think he's sick. But he is. Very sick.

That we know I said.

No, I mean descending into full dementia. Rapidly. Even with all the depravity I've seen you knew there was a high level of cunning at work. His size got him to the top back in the old days, but his smarts kept him there. But now...

She rolled her head to spit again.

Now things are spiraling. He is having visions. God is appearing before him and has told him the end is here. Not near but here. He was up all-night drinking and smoking white horse. God told him his son would return tomorrow. Jesus is coming tomorrow. Annie's eighteenth birthday.

Not very thoughtful of God to give such short notice I said.

Annie smiled weakly and looked up at Mari.

I like him.

He's ok Mari said.

Do you know where she's at this minute? I asked.

No. But I need to tell you what is happening so you understand.

The priest told Harold you were coming.

Mari looked at me. My eyes narrowed. Fucking priest.

And why would he do that? How did he do that? And why would you think he would help you?

Because Harold had something on him, just like he does on me.

A horn from the same part of town blared out three long blasts.

We must hurry she said. The gatherers want to start drinking and won't be far up the road. You better move that big one.

I ran from the sage and pulled the fat bastard around the berm and out of sight. It took all my strength. Burning about the priest. Stay focused and deal with him later. I crested the berm next to criss and cross and looked for movement. You could hear shouting in town. The dirt road was quiet for now.

I sprinted back and Mari nodded at me.

Annie is going to make it up to the Mission she said.

What?

Trust us. Annie get going.

She managed to stand one-legged.

Hold on I said. I cut two cloth strips from the bottom of her torn long skirt. I wrapped one tightly around her bad knee. The other I ripped in half and wrapped the knuckles of both hands.

If you have to crawl this will help I said.

Do you know where your heart pendant is?

She instinctively touched her neck.

Frida has it. She lowered her head, tears dripping from her chin.

Bring Jess out of there. Please. I don't care what happens to me.

We will bring her out and come for you Mari said. Now go.

She wiped tears with the back of her hand and started the climb.

We ran for the tunnel door and pulled criss and cross into the dirt.

I really hate this my love, but I think we need to borrow this fashionable Hag attire for our next leg of this infernal adventure. And while doing this maybe you can help me understand why Annie is crawling back to that treasonous fuck of a priest.

Assuming you can talk while retching of course.

God these two stunk. They would actually smell better in a few days.

What does Harold have on the priest? And who is Frida? We were pulling off their cowboy boots, standard issue for all Hags since the supply was inexhaustible. It was Texas after all.

Frida was Jess's best friend. And Annie's eyes in the harem. And the daughter of our priest.

Well God damn. We need just one more mystery daughter reveal and we have a trifecta. I can just throw one over each shoulder and head into the Scald dragging a cripple with a white cat on my head.

But you said Frida was and not is and I don't think I like that.

She was bent over the giggler's boots like a farrier, pulling.

Frida is dead. Annie told Frida on the way out of Harold's basement to get Jess and run. Hide and run out through the tunnels when they had a chance. Annie was going to drug the guards and they were going to make a run for the Mission. Harold got suspicious and sent a guard to watch Jess but she was gone. They caught Frida and took her to Harold.

When we heard the horn, I presume.

He had Franklin go get Annie and drag her back. They killed Frida in front of her and were dragging Annie out here to kill. Harold wanted it out of sight because the peasants would not be happy he killed their Healer.

I had my foot on prayer boys' loin cup for boot-pulling leverage. I gave it a hard kick.

So Frida knew her Father was the priest.

We were unlacing bloody leg chaps.

No. Annie just said someone there would help them and someone else was coming to get them out.

The leather arm sheathes covered from elbow to shoulder and had to be shucked from the top down to remove.

So why did they have to run? She knew we were coming.

Harold will tell the town tonight that tomorrow is the rapture...

And - I finished the thought - Harold's revised Hagian Bible says a Virgin must hang on the cross before Jesus will return. Let me guess who that would be.

Yep.

So, they caught Frida but Jess got away. Did Annie have a clue where she would hide?

We had wrangled the dirty desert camo pants off and were hitching them on.

She said start at Levi's.

We rolled them to get the shirts off and shrugged the smelly camo on. We started lacing the thigh chaps. The boots would stay.

Because that was her best option in the tunnel?

Yes. But also, because her and Levi are in love.

I stopped and look at her as she rolled an arm leather up and grabbed the drifter hat. She propped it on her helmet and drew the string and tapped the top, all while looking at me with a bemused grin.

I pulled on my arm leathers and put on the stupid hat.

There is good news she said with a sunny lilt.

Oh good!

The priest told Harold we would be in the tunnels tomorrow night. He bought us a day to find the girls.   It was his only choice. He's probably watching us now. But he couldn't have seen what they did to Frida. I hope.

My pants were high water, hers rolled up into cuffs. We looked like space cowboys with hand-me down pants.

And smelled like carbon-titanium shit.

We were ready.

If it couldn't get any better she said.

Hell.

Harold will tell the town tonight Rebel Angels are coming to take Jess.

Naturally! So, we have not only the Hag Army, but now the Hag Nation looking for us. And Jess, who won't stick out at all in that fucking white dress. And they aren't terribly motivated or anything because if Jesus doesn't get his living dead girl he takes his miracles and goes home. Leaving them in this shithole to be eaten by an insane giant, that's all.

You are so brilliant my love.

If you just had some ass-less chaps these getups would be perfect I said.

She laughed as we dropped into the tunnel.

Hagtown dark was darker, I was sure.

Between candles was a black zone that felt like swimming in ink. You could see the pinpoint of a candle ahead but it was encased in black. You walked in ink and suddenly bright. Pupils like balloons then pop. The light seemed to huddle to stay safe. We stopped on the edge of each light huddle and listened for guard noises.

The smell was like any tunnel, earthy and rooty and damp. The candles were about one hundred paces apart. I was leading so Mari was shielded from attack and could retaliate.

She had her palm on my lower back and guided me around hairy face lying in the liquid black past the second candle. The dirt was sticky. The fresh death metallic smell was stirring the ink.

We made it to candle seven when a faint shout froze us. We waited.

I figured the guard post at the junction would be well lit. Visualizing the cement road above us I guessed it was next.

We were about to be out of the ink and exposed. Hopefully the getups would buy us time to close the gap and attack. I would lower my head and let the drifter hat cover my face, buying time to close in. We had left the battle straps and crucifix's behind, so the getup only bought a few seconds. But that was enough.

The junction came into view. It was rounded out with rooty walls. Two big wood chairs in the middle facing down our tunnel. Not fancy but effective. One guard to fight, one to run for help.

No guards I whispered.

Let's just walk straight through like we belong she said.

I guessed criss and cross were supposed to be on duty, but couldn't resist a go at Annie. They should have. They would have lived until now.

I sped up and we walked through the junction. I glanced right down the chopping block tunnel curving left in the distance. Tunnel of horror. Had a red aura - or maybe just my imagination. Harold's tunnel was on the back left and curved left. We hugged the wall and moved fast. We started seeing little plastic squares on the tunnel floor, stuck in the dirt. Fingernails and toenails. The flesh couriers were no doubt instructed to clean the catch before delivery. Mari didn't need to palm my back anymore but did anyway.

I was just hoping we didn't see any snakes.

Candle sconces were now on every vertical timber. A haunted house vibe but good vision. Wax spidered down the timbers, growing deeper as it cooled, forming wax stalactites. Vanilla, blue, red, green wax - flickering like a kaleidoscope as we kept easing left and slightly down. I focused on the furthest point ahead. Harold's door may have a guard. Should have a guard. Probably basement side of the door with a peephole and secret knock or something. Maybe you had to recite a Bible verse. The one about keep knocking and he'll let you in - or maybe that was the old song I hear you knockin' but you can't come in.

We stopped to listen.

Mari was watching our flank. We could hear voices ahead but not what they were saying. Mari's hand on my back. Blade in my right hand, Mari's in the left. Our feet shimmering dirty red. My high-waters were showing some red ankle. Hands looked dipped in blood.

I began moving again. With the Festival about to start the odds were in our favor. Everyone would be up top getting ready to party. Only Harold knew we were coming through the tunnels. Tomorrow. Would he take this chance? Could be a trap. But more likely he told criss and cross to watch the tunnel and they cocked it up - a couple of assholes who had fallen so low on the pecking order they were relegated to tunnel duty at the start of the year's biggest party.

A recess in the wall ahead. Voices were getting louder. Ten paces out I could see the edge of a steel door. I moved to the recess edge and lowered down to have a look. There was a simple wood crucifix near the top and a peep hole just underneath. The pull handle had been sawed off. Something splattered on the door bottom. Voices behind it. The latch was on our side - we needed to be on the other side. I duck-walked over with Mari in tow. I glanced on down the tunnel towards Levi's. It was straight for about fifty paces then veered left. If they came out we wouldn't be able to close the gap.

We needed to listen.

I swearin' on my Bible those two dumb-fucks ain't at they posts.

Yous probably right. But they was headin' out yonder the fence with the bitch so not likes anybody gonna get by em'. And with the Ox and Wild Man even less likely. Rebel Angels ain't comin till' tomorrow anyway. You ain't very bright.

I don't think they's comin' at all.

You best lower your voice fuckwit. If the boss hear that shit I will be eatin' your dumb ass for supper tonight.

He ain't hearin' shit. He be upside bustin' heads till his little darlin' turns up. Too bad we ain't eat'n her.

Blasphemous fuck you is.

They chuckled like pervs.

I cocked the drifter hat to the side and tilted my head back as Mari leaned forward,

They aren't going anywhere I whispered. Let's move on.

She pivoted and we moved slowly.

Levis' door would be locked. Probably not two guards but maybe one.

I glanced back every few seconds and my ears were straining for that door latch.

Moving fast now. Levi's place was maybe two hundred paces so wouldn't be long.

I wondered if Jess had found Levi and if she would tell him the plan to flee out the tunnel. She almost certainly would. She was a teenage girl in love.

Mari stopped.

Levi's door was staring at us at the end of the tunnel. The tunnel narrowed gradually leaving no place to hide on the sides of the door. The turn to Franklin's must have been just before it. We could make out what looked like an identical crucifix to Harold's and no doubt a peephole below it. They could see us right now.

The odds are they aren't looking until somebody knocks I whispered.

Yes. And if they are looking standing here won't do us any good she said.

We started moving again, faster.

I knew what she was going to do and it was our only option.

Ten paces out from the door was the left to Franklin's. A dead end.

We reached the door and she let her hat fall back and holstered her blade and we listened. Nothing. She pulled off her helmet and handed it to me. She shook her hair. I crouched down peering between her legs. She stepped up to the peep hole to hide her shimmer. She would step back against the wall as the door opened and I would spring up to cut him or them down.

She rapped three times. I knew the peeper was getting her best poor wittle me pouty face. It would work on me.

Nothing.

She rapped again.

Nothing.

Then something.

The latch was slowly scratching metal to metal and then a solid click.

The door creaked and Mari slid left. Halfway open I grabbed the bottom and jerked it hard.

Jessica was standing in peasant clothes. She had been crying.

Time slowed.

I took it all in. An arm extended from the right had a tight grip on her left wrist. Above the arm off her left shoulder were two tall soldiers. Four paces back, battle straps up.

Off her right shoulder were Franklin and Smilin' Pat.

Rising up behind her was Harold.

His eyes were looking in two different directions that seem to merge into a beam directed at me. His head had a quick jerk like he had water in his ear. He opened his mouth to speak through teeth that looked like jumbled piano keys.

Propping Jess up in the door was a mistake.

My blade moving faster than I ever remember. The hand had released her but I took all the fingers off but the thumb in the same instant my left pulled her by the collar and yanked her violently out of the doorway, using her weight as leverage to step through. My front foot slipped on a finger and

104

blood spray as I reached back with my left without looking and slammed the door.

Everyone had moved back, mouths hanging open, except for Harold.

Levi was kneeling on the floor in front of Harold, facing me. Harold raised a gun and pointed it at my face.

I told you Rebel Angels were the greatest tricksters! He laughed. There was flopping around and moaning with no fingers on my right but I didn't look.

He turned his head left but kept his eyes on me - I think - and told the two tall ones to get to the East gate and secure the tunnel exit.

I want both alive and unharmed he said as they backed up the stairs, never taking their eyes off me.

Another mistake. I knew he didn't want me and Mari dead. At least yet.

That was impressive demon. Now take off that uniform you dishonor and let us see your true evil. Let us see the suit of Satan.

I was considering the gun. I trusted he had tested it. He was about five paces from me in the middle of the basement so a good chance of hitting an eye.

I glanced right to see whose finger I was standing on. It was the unfortunately named Lucky. He was banging his head against the floor with both arms under him trying to squeeze away the pain. He rolled his face towards me with eyes shut impossibly tight. His silver metal prosthetic nose had gotten misaligned with all the head banging and was around by his left ear. His pig snout nose was raw looking and snotty and sucking in air. He was moaning for someone to help him.

Pat help poor Lucky said Harold. Take him upstairs and put a tourniquet on and splash it with hooch. Get him good and drunk and we'll fix him up later.

Smilin' Pat never took his eyes off me as he and his big chompers side-stepped around to Lucky. He helped him to his feet and they trailed a bloody mess to the back wall and up the stairs.

Now just me and the big three.

Levi was looking at the ground. Franklin was sneering at me.

Out of those clothes said Franklin.

Levi looked up. His eyes revealed heartbreak.

I pushed the hat off and reached up with my sword hand to roll the leather sleeve down my left arm. I moved methodically, never taking my eyes off of Harold, always focused on the position of the of blade in my right hand. The pile of smell soon lay beside me. I stood before them a crimson shimmer.

I told you boys. I told you the Rebel Angels were real. His voice was a whispering awe.

I looked at Franklin, then Levi. Very different souls looking out. The stairwell, blood trickling down the bottom step. The earthy tunnel smell succumbing to the blood and Hag stench. Lucky cried out upstairs.

This is God's plan said Harold. These boys might have been my Cain and Abel, but God saved Levi here for a grander plan. He allowed his heart to desire the Virgin, but did not give him her body. She is on this earth to die for us. A pure Virgin daughter of the infidels. To die so he will return. And you and your demon bitch will die next to her. Two demon thieves who tried to steal our redemption. It has been foretold. He is returning. We will ascend with our Savior, while you descend to burn for eternity, sent to the flames by the sword of Jesus himself.

The gun was his lecture finger, stabbing at me on the high points.

In a burst I dove right, headlong into a left shoulder roll, lunging back left for the stairwell as I hit my feet. Harold was cursing. As my foot hit the bottom stair a shot rang out. The sound bounced around the basement in a deafening pulse causing even more cursing. I reached the top of the stairs in two bounds and slung the heavy wood door shut. I slid a heavy straight back chair under the handle as Smilin' Pat rounded a corner, blade in hand. He saw me and ran for the front door screaming God help me.

I sank a blade in his ear and he fell chompers down dead.

A cursing fist battered the basement door. Harold was screaming spawn of hell! Spawn of hell! Then boots rumbling down the steps and the tunnel door opening and closing.

I knew Mari had enough time to get out. If they caught her they would wish they hadn't.

I listened. I could hear the festival crowd in the distance.

I went looking for Lucky down the hallway. I found him on a tattered sofa in a room with a single candle. He recoiled in horror, shaking with shock. He was soaked in hooch and blood. Pat had just skipped the tourniquet and poured hooch on him. Probably kicked his hand. Let him bleed then shank him in the back and slap a tourniquet on his arm.

I was letting her go he said.

I know. You would have lost your arm and bled out. I'm going to take off your belt.

He seemed stunned at my voice. And words.

I pulled his belt out then cut one of his arm sheaths lengthwise. I folded it and wrapped his wrist. I pulled his knife from its holster and stabbed it through the wrap and twisted. I looped the belt over his head and placed his arm in the sling.

Keep pressure on the knife I said. Let off every now and then.

I've seen you do good things for people in this town. That has saved your life today. But if you throw in with Harold you will die with him, do you understand?

Yes. He trembled.

I slid his metallic nose back into place and gave him a drink from my canteen.

Can you tell me anything I don't already know?

Franklin is plotting against Harold he said. And Levi. He has some soldiers behind him. I wouldn't go along is why Pat was going to let me die. And he thinks I'm a Muslim. Harold would have caught wind of this before but he's crazy now. You aren't a demon, are you?

No. A man just like you.

He looked at my shimmering blade arm.

If you hightail outta here go wait by the well at the Mission on the hill. Don't go in the mission, just wait by the well. Take some grub if you got any. Find something to cover yourself with because your probably in shock or gonna be. There's a white cat that hangs around the well and I want you to be nice to him. Feed him. Wait seven days and I will come to help you. Do you understand?

Yes. Thank you.

You know what Harold is going to do at dawn don't you?

Yes, I said. Only it's not going to happen. This town is going to explode, so do as I say.

I left through the kitchen and out the back door.

I ran across the dirt yard and into the cul de sac. Nobody in sight. I could see the fires in the square and hear the din. The air was still hot but would drop soon. Harold's house was quiet. If Mari got in she would be watching Levi's from the front door and have already seen me coming. No movement yet. Worrisome. I stopped at the front sidewalk leading to the front door and waited. One minute. Two. At five I went to the front door and tried. Locked. I circled right to get a view of the clear window upstairs. Dark. If she got in that tunnel door she would be here. Her options would have been back to the East gate or the chopping block - or Franklin's. She would have had to double-back in the tunnel and could have run into Harold. I ran back across the cul de sac to Franklin's and stood in line of sight of the peephole, waiting.

A minute passed and I heard the latch. The door opened and Franklin was standing there with his arm around Jess. My blood ran cold.

Soldiers began running from the sides of the house to surround me. Maybe thirty in all. Many were loudly praying. One stopped suddenly - gawking at me - and several bowling pinned him.

Here's what you is gonna do devil spawn, if you ever wanna see your devil bitch again said the pederast. You will walk down to the square with these boys here. You will do as your told when we get to the party. Do you understand?

Are you hurt Jessica? I asked.

He squeezed her shoulder and put his forehead on her head next to her ear.

I'm fine she said, more firmly than I expected.

Where is my partner?

Oh, she's in good hands he laughed. Laughter in the dark behind him.

She's about thirty years too old for you Franklin. And know this pederast. If she's harmed you will be the first to suffer and last to die.

He jerked his arm from Jess and started out the door, hand on blade.

Franklin! roared Harold from back of the room.

He stepped back in and Harold was saying something I couldn't hear.

Franklin turned back to me.

She has not been harmed devil. God has a grand plan for you. And Jesus will deal with you and your bitch at dawn.

Again - plans. Enemy.

Dumbass.

I backed away and turned with my smelly entourage down the boulevard. They kept their distance in a big moving circle and stared like slack-jawed yokels. I was guessing Harold's bumpkin guards were among this ring of mouth-breathers, having abandoned their post and forcing Mari to Franklin's child trap. The rest of this bunch was probably holed up at Franklin's plotting the coup by drawing in the dirt or something. Harold would have come in behind Mari with the gun and she was trapped.

Harold's mental breakdown was a stroke of luck. Any harm to us would ruin his dramatic theater and might screw up the rapture. I glanced back at Jess. She looked like she was gonna punch Franklin in the face. I liked her already.

I would now be paraded in front of ten thousand peasants to show Harold's power. He can capture Rebel Angels! They would gasp and pray and some would faint. They would smell awful.

We had until dawn to come up with something or the three of us were going to die on a cross.

Harold led our procession towards the Square, Franklin on his right flank. No Levi. In his place was Hoss the Shorty. It was hard to see the nasty little General but he had a signature cackle-laugh oft heard from that one kid who liked to burn ant hills. The top of his head was about Harold's belt line so he had to be the butt - or head - of many jokes. His big ears only made it worse.

If they got over Red Rebel Angel shock some of the less drunk townspeople might notice I was strapped with three blades. But the strange was a way of life here and questions were not.

The boulevard concrete was hogged and sagging from decades of hammer sun and fracking quakes. The once verdant road verge was rock hard and lumpy brown. The Aristo and Soldier neighborhoods were nearly deserted. The rapture party was no doubt mandatory, but some more worldly Aristo's were likely hiding out. Hooch and Hag soldiers was a volatile mix. It made sense to steer clear. Jesus will still find me in the closet and I don't have to smell those god-awful peasants would have been a logical thought process, as far as that line of thinking goes.

Harold was a striding giant in a hurry so everyone else was damn near jogging. Hoss was running, trying to look like he wasn't. The circle of dunces were eyeing me but kept glancing towards the Square. It was like the Fair midway, loud and bright and clangy. Mari and I would be the main attractions all night as a fumey swell of drunks pushed to the stage for a chance to witness the Rebel Angels up close.

Aristo huddles had convened on the outskirts, drinking and laughing with soldier bodyguards lurking.

When they saw me, they backed up or fell to their knees. There were spontaneous screams and prayers.

Harold save us!

No fear my friends! he bellowed. The Rebel Angel obeys me!

Hoss let out a winded cackle.

The crowd thickened as we rolled towards the square, pulling the huddles in our wake. The entrance gate was huge telephone poles with a message carved into a massive timber crossbeam - "Great is our LORD and abundant in power his understanding is beyond measure". Youngsters were clinging to the poles and crossbeam to get a look. One had a leg hanging over the L in LORD. We walked under our ORD into a sea of humanity.

An electric murmur cascaded across the Square as word spread. The dunce's pushed and implored and barked commands as we entered the main space. The brown sea parted, a stunned silence with all eyes on me. People were dropping their cups and rending their shirts. Hands over mouths. Covering the eyes of children.

A line of soldiers stood before the stage. We arrived front and center and a wailing began, silenced by my gaze as I slowly turned.

Like any preacher worth his salt, Harold had them where he wanted them.

He raised a huge hand for silence.

I saw the gun grip peeking from his battle strap.

My friends! I stand before you your humble servant. On this night, only hours from the return of our Savior, I bring you proof of God's almighty power. Behold the Rebel Angel.

Someone near the front fainted. A cacophony of prayers filled the Square.

See the flames of hell shining through?

See the head of the man and the body of the beast?

See Satan's evil technology imprisoning his mind?

He rose to a crescendo, and the crowd responded.

He raised both hands.

God has used me to shield you from this demon.

But he did not come alone.

Oh no Father no!

Behold the bride of Satan. He swept his arm across the stage for effect.

A sheet of crinkled and curled plywood was laid down and there stood Mari in all her red-hot glory.

The crowd gasped.

Mari and I had a long look. I would bring up the bride of Satan thing later.

This has been foretold! He boomed. Technology is the destructor, and only Jesus can save the few who heeded the warning. You are the few. You are the chosen. We ascend to eternal life at dawn!

The crowd bounced with hoorays and shouts of joy.

So, drink my friends! This is your last night in this forsaken world. At dawn our Savior will strike these two demon thieves down. They came to steal our Virgin - but instead, they will be cast back to the flames dragging their bowels.

And our Virgin will take us home.

The crowd roared and surged towards the stage, the soldiers pushing them back. Mari was glancing at a big warrior to her right, cradling a little girl in a huge arm with his fist turned down, blade in hand pointing at the floor. He held a rope in his free hand attached in a daisy chain around the necks of a small boy and girl in his shadow, maybe four years old. They were holding hands and trying not to cry. The girl in his arms was crying dirt-streaked tears as the big man rocked and bounced her in faux comfort, eyeing Mari with a three-tooth grin.

Harold jumped from the stage and pushed into my circle.

You see the precious children demon. They will ascend to heaven in the arms of Christ either way. You and the bitch will be strapped to your cross to await our Lord. If you do not obey, those little throats will be slit. I will make you drink their blood.

I said nothing, just a blank stare into his crazed eyes.

Men began setting up ladders across the stage. Harold was saying something to Mari. Probably the same speech I just got. She had the same reaction as I and glanced at me several times. Harold was going to keep us apart, maybe the only smart thing he had done all day.

Our crosses were dragged out and propped at an angle on the ladders. Harold told Franklin to bring me up on stage. Battle straps were brought out and laid across each cross arm. The horde was now taking in hooch two-fisted and began to gather at the stage to watch the spectacle. Will the demons fight back?

The crosses were the same black railroad timbers in the tunnel, spiked together so the crucified leaned out chest first.

Franklin decided I was first.

You know what to do spawn. Do it now. Remember the precious kiddies.

Aren't you gonna strap me up Franklin? Everybody in hell knows you like to tie up men with leather. Maybe I should be face down on the cross.

Snorts of laughter that died when he pulled his blade.

He took a step towards me, rocking it. But then his face calmed and he stepped back, laughing.

The Devil is so full of tricks he said. Tempt me all you will, nothing changes as he holstered his blade.

I climbed the beam and laid back, arms out. The battle straps were wrapped from wrist to just above the elbow and ankles to mid-calf. The men were afraid of touching me. One on the ladder and one on the ground pulled the strap down and then under up and over. It was tight. The head-hole in the strap was secured with a leather tie. I had cocked my right elbow a little as they wrapped to try and create some leverage.

The loin cup happened to fall across my ankles facing the crowd. They were pointing and laughing.

The strapping crew moved to Mari.   I watched as they tied her in. Her wraps went further up the arms and legs. She wouldn't be able to move at all.

Harold was front and center stage watching.

Try to get some sleep he bellowed at us, to the delight of the crowd.

He jumped from the stage into the crowd. They surged back as his men followed, pushing and shoving. The children were handed down by Three Tooth and he and Franklin took up the rear. The pedo looked back and gave me a throat-slash.

Harold and his men took tables near the back of the Square to wait and drink. His harem was lined up behind him, faces covered in veils. No white dress.

I closed my eyes. The stench was thick as I breathed deeply. I could feel the putrid air in my mouth, down the windpipe into the lungs, like a bad cigar fighting a dirty diaper. I could feel my pulse against the leather. I looked at the big gate at the back of the Square that opened into the Scald. It was the familiar telephone poles and crossbeam but had cyclone fencing layered across it nearly to the crossbeam. It wasn't used much. There was a normal sized wood door at one edge for guards to come and go. That was our direct path out of here. The Scald seemed very inviting. We had taken a huge risk. I knew Mari was thinking the same thing. I opened my eyes and she was watching me. I winked at her.

He's praying! Someone yelled.

We only needed two things: Jessica between us and one hand free. The first was certain - the second was not.

———————————

My body was trapped but my mind was flying.

Two soldiers were between us milling around Jess's cross that lay flat on the stage. They had succumbed to drink and were playing grab-ass.

The seething mass of smell had fights breaking out, those in various levels of passed out, puking, and a few praying at the foot of the stage. Someone threw a hooch cup at Mari but missed. Harold dispatched two big soldiers to beat the the tosser senseless.

We were untouchable now, but when Jesus said never mind at dawn they were going to try and spill our guts on the stage. When that didn't work they would try beheading. That could work.

We didn't have long until dawn. I looked at Mari.

I mouthed "Levi" and she nodded. I jerked my head down and glanced behind Jess's cross. She would be propped up right in front of the chopping block and the tunnel trap door. She nodded again.

With maybe an hour to go the party was still going strong. The smell of hooch mingled with the stench. Some had blacked out and been dragged to the fringes. There was groping and pinching and dancing. The devout at the front were ignoring the debauchery, some rocking in prayer and some asleep on the ground. Puke puddles. God was not going to be happy with all the puking at the pearly gates.

Harold stared my way. I had not seen him drinking.

Franklin was drunk and near a bunch of kids sleeping in some straw.

Jess would be coming soon. And Levi - I hoped. But hope was a poor battle strategy. I had wiggled some room with my elbow and could turn my hand up. Harold staring had me moving very slowly. I needed this arm free whether Levi showed or not. We were counting on his love for Jess and smarts. No Jesus opened Franklin's coup window. He and Jess would die anyway. So, throw in with the Rebel Angels and at least die defending your woman.

It was a clear and beautiful night with a big bright moon now fading on the edges. The air was cool. The night black was beginning to soften. Harold stood and yelled for Franklin.

Franklin stumbled away from the kids to get his orders. He turned and said something to a group of soldiers and they fell in behind him, wading through the bodies and the sick then disappearing at the gate where I had arrived.

I worked my elbow. I could turn my forearm and had started pushing and pulling against the leather. If I could get my arm back through and lean there might be enough room to pull free. Just one hand and one blade is all I needed.

Raise the thieves! boomed Harold.

The dazed and weary crowd began to stir.

I pushed my right hand back partially out of the leather. Soldiers jumped on stage and raised us upright. The base was dropped into holes cut into the stage and thunked firmly against the earth underneath. Jarring as hell but put me closer to the stage.

I was tilted forward, pressure on all the leather straps.

It wasn't long before Franklin was back at the entrance, waiting with his entourage for the signal from Harold.

It is time my people! boomed Harold. Cleanse your eyes of the Rebel Angels, and witness the Virgin!

While we were being tilted the still standing had been reaching to help up the downed, propping them up on wobbly legs to see the demons in full glory. They looked like hell after a night of swilling hooch.

Heaven was going to look like a pirate Sunday morning in Tortuga.

As they looked away from me towards the entrance I worked on the leather.

Franklin marched in with Jess in tow, a soldier escort on either side. She was wearing the white dress.

Several soldiers shuffled behind her at a reverent distance.

No Levi.

He had to be part of this. Where the hell was he.

The crowd was quiet. They parted for the procession.

Jess looked at Mari and then me. Her eyes were calm on rosy cheeks as she moved gracefully through the horde. The white dress was plain but spotless, adorned only with the heart pendant.

Franklin stepped on the stage and held down his hand. She ignored it and stepped up, taking care with her dress hem.

She turned back to face the crowd. Many fell to their knees.

Harold stepped up and stood beside her. He towered above her, his dark and hairy mass dwarfing her pure white grace.

The cross lay behind her, huge and white. She showed no emotion.

The white dress seemed to glow against the brown sea of humanity.

Before we prepare the Virgin for our Lord, you must now witness the failed work of these demons.

That did not sound good.

Mari and I looked at each other then back at Harold.

I was pushing and pulling on the leather trying to look like I wasn't. Sweat burned my eyes.

More soldiers marched through the gate. They hurried through the murmuring crowd and I saw Levi in the center. His face was bloodied and he was limping. They pushed him up the steps, arms roped to his sides. He was forced to his knees in front of Jess.

They looked at each other like nobody else was around.

My beloved son Levi, boomed Harold. He loves this Virgin. For this he is blameless. He obeyed God's will and did not defile her holy purity. But then the demons arrived, planting seeds of evil in his mind. Weakened by his wanton desires, he allowed a seed of evil to take hold. He plotted against me. Against our town. Against the Lord Jesus Christ. He sought to kill me and flee with his Virgin prize.

Shouting and crying.

Harold raised his hand.

Do not despair! I know you love Levi. I love Levi. And more than any of us, Jesus loves Levi. He long ago accepted the Lord Jesus Christ into his heart. His sins were washed clean in the blood of the lamb. He will ascend with us into heaven.

Cries of relief and praise.

Levi was still looking at Jess. He looked up at Mari, then me. That looked like defiance.

Harold raised his hand.

Levi had the honor of driving the stakes. But his sin has a cost. The honor will now fall to my eldest son Franklin.

The crowd was silent.

Harold looked at the sky to see if the time was nigh. The stars were fading from black into blue and gone in the first red hint of the sun.

Jessica my angel. It is time to mount the cross he said.

Levi tried to rise but Harold's hand stopped him.

I couldn't get my elbow clear of the leather.

She turned and walked to the big white cross, carefully sitting in position and laying back to spread her arms. She placed her feet on a small foothold nailed six feet from the bottom, and her hands in leather loops. The two drunk guards carefully raised her up and waited as another slid ladders into place to prop it at an angle. Franklin would climb these to hammer in the hand spikes.

Three small children came from the back, each carrying a single black barn spike. They lined them up at the foot of the cross and ran to stand behind Harold.

An old man followed with a small sledge hammer painted white. He stood it on edge in front of the spikes.

My shoulder was nearly dislocated but my elbow was moving.

Franklin stepped up to the hammer.

He kneeled and placed the first spike against her feet. Jess did not move or make a sound, watching Levi. He laid the hammer head sideways on the head of the spike. A trickle of blood rolled down her toes. He looked at me out of the corner of his eye and smiled.

Let us pray my children! boomed Harold.

They all bowed their heads. Except Levi.

We were in big trouble.

Out of the Dying Pan into the Fire
10

Harold was praying. The Square was silent, heads bowed. One did not speak or look up when Harold was praying.

Levi was on his knees behind Franklin. Harold was beside him, one arm raised, face to the sky. He put all his power into this final prayer, and it was something. You could have heard it deep in the Scald.

My arm was aching and my shoulder was moving in ways not intended. The raising of the cross had shifted my weight forward against the straps - made worse by my supply pack pushing me even further forward. It was nearly empty but the steel canteen was on the right, becoming a wedge between my shoulder and the cross on the arm I was trying to free.

Harold had shown a flair for the dramatic with this whole production. Jess would be staked and raised as the centerpiece, Levi on his knees bowing before her, Harold to his left and Franklin to his right. The three stake-bearers were huddled behind Harold one little girl was watching me.

And Levi was watching me. Harold has a hand on his shoulder to make sure he didn't get any ideas.

Lord God we give you this Virgin to prove our devotion.

She shall be the first to ascend with your Son our Savior Jesus Christ.

We ask for your divine mercy to save us from this fallen world.

Sweat was burning my eyes as I pulled with all I had. I was looking down trying to clear my eyes as I leaned left. My elbow was nearly out. I was sure Franklin was gonna look up any moment, but he kept his head down. The blood excited him.

Harold was rising to a dramatic ending. I looked up, blinking hard. The little girl and Levi were not looking at me. Something behind me. I look at Mari and she was watching behind me. She looked at me and winked.

Jesus, hear the voices of your children and return to us now.

He began the 23rd Psalm and the crowd joined in.

The Lord is my shepherd, I shall not want...

Something bumped the back of my cross.

He maketh me to lie down in green pastures, he leadeth me beside the still waters...

The leather at my wrist suddenly felt loose. The feeling spread across the wrap as it flayed open. The cool air poured over my sweat soaked arm as the leather hung free.

The little girl was pointing at me and saying something.

Levi's eyes were wide but he dared not move.

He restoreth my soul....I had a blade flat against the cross sliding it down the leather to free my left arm. Suddenly my legs came free and I swung around to the blade, hugging it to my chin.

He leadeth me in the paths of righteousness for his name's sake...

At righteousness, the blade sliced through and I fell into a crouch facing the back. No screams of terror yet.

Yea, though I walk through the valley of the shadow of death...

I walked straight to Mari's cross as my rescuer jumped from the back of the stage, a black duster flaring as he hit the ground and disappeared.

I will fear no evil, for thou art with me, thy rod and thy staff they comfort me...

The ladder was close and I freed her right arm. I reached around her waist and cut her legs free as she sliced the left strap. I let her go and she landed in a crouch, pulling her big blade free. We moved towards Jess.

The little girl was tugging on Harold's pants.

Jess jumped from the cross and I half-caught her in one arm. Levi didn't move. The crying girl was tugging Harold's pants and saying, "Father the Devil is loose".

Harold suddenly trailed off at presence of mine enemies and looked down at the little girl then turned towards us.

No! he roared. The children fell backwards from the power as the crowd was momentarily stunned.

Soldiers!

A big explosion above the main gate sent a shock wave through the crowd. All eyes turned to see as they recoiled and fell. A popper.

Jess and I ran for the trap door with Levi right behind, leaving Harold's hand hanging suspended as he stared at the main gate, expecting hell's legions to burn through.

The Square went from stunned to pandemonium. Hell was invading.

Then another popper, almost to the ground, blowing a hole in the guard door, shooting splinter shrapnel and knocking swathes of the fleeing crowd to the ground. The smoke rose above the cross-timber and from it burst a drone, full speed, circling the square and diving at the crowd.

Harold hadn't moved.

I cut Levi free and handed him the blade. I told him the plan and we dropped a ladder down through the trap door. He and Jess climbed down and clunked the trap door shut. I heard the ladder wedge against the wood.

Mari was between me and Harold. He was watching the drone.

Mari come on I said. We gotta go.

I knew how bad she wanted him. So did I. But not the time. He had the gun.

Baby, look at me.

She turned back.

We will get our chance. We need to go, now.

She turned back to Harold as she started moving towards me. We bounded off the back of stage. The shadows were long and deep as we made our way through the holding cell maze and into a narrow street. People were running in all directions. The shacks were wall to wall as we ran looking for the first path east. We found a narrow alley that looked and smelled like an open latrine and we took it, trying to stay on the high side. We came out onto the boulevard into the last of the screaming crowd. They saw us and repelled away causing more trampling and stumbling. We fell in behind the last of them like cowboys following a panicked herd. The little crying girl Three Tooth was going to kill was in the street, left behind. Mari scooped her up and told her it was going to be ok. When we got close to the tunnel shack I grabbed a young woman from behind and told her to stop. She was wetting herself in terror.

We will not harm you I said, if you take this child to her Mother.

Mari kissed the child and handed her over and we disappeared into the shack. We dropped through a trapdoor onto a rickety ladder into the junction. No guards. We ran through the chopping tunnel. We had to hurry. If lucky the Square would clear and we could get out through the blasted hole in the fence. Harold and the soldiers would be recovering about now.

Levi was in front and Jess behind the ladder. Nobody tried to break it he said.

We pulled it clear of the door and I climbed up to look out. The Square was quiet. The drone was gone. I slowly stepped up the ladder, my head on a swivel, short blade over my face. I rose over the altar and Harold was gone. The Square was empty.

Come on I said.

We climbed out and jumped from the stage. We sidestepped bodies like running through a mine field. I reached the hole and checked the outside. All clear. Mari went through first then Jess and Levi.

Demon!

Franklin. Walking towards me from the stage with Hoss and Three Tooth and a couple more. He had what looked like Harold's gun aimed as he walked. Hoss was also pointing a gun - looked like a 45. The longer I waited the better their odds so I dove through the hole as two shots rang out. One hit my butt and bounced and the other missed, barely. I felt the slug graze my neck as it whistled through the hole.

Mari had everyone running into the Scald. I came up in full sprint and was about to catch them. Mari and I were safe from rear shots so I tried to stay between the hole and Jess. Mari fell back doing the same. Jess had her dress pulled up with both hands, running barefoot. Levi had no shirt over his camo pants and leather and cowboy boots and was running awkwardly behind her. It wasn't exactly a sprint but would have to do. We were almost out of water, heading into the Scald as the sun rose. Barefoot, topless and nearly out of water. Awesome.

Four more shots rang out. One was either damned good or lucky and bounced off the back of Mari's helmet. She let out a string of curse words that made Jess giggle. I wondered about Shorty and his decades in the army. He had to be good at something to make up for his shortcomings.

I caught up to Mari and she looked over and stopped me suddenly, hand on my arm. I didn't like the look.

Niki. Baby your hurt.

Jess and Levi stopped and turned.

Then I saw the blood on my arm dripping into the sand. I felt the burn on my neck, like an icicle under the skin. My right eye was blurring. That little rat bastard hadn't missed at the gate. One small place on the side of the neck and he hit it on a moving target in poor light while walking and shooting.

She had her hand over the wound.

She told Levi to cut off two strips from the bottom of Jess's dress. She folded one into a thick square and had Levi hold it on the wound.

It's a deep graze baby. Passed on through luckily. It's not the big vein but I don't have to tell you that's a bad place to get shot.

I'll remind Shorty how inconsiderate he was when I slice the little shit in half.

She wrapped the second strip around my neck three times and tied it off. I saw the fear.

It's just a flesh wound my love.

Don't turn your head if you can help it. Straight ahead and no talking either, which I know will be damn near impossible for you. We gotta go.

She gave me a kiss.

Levi was making some shoes for Jess with a leg chap. He cut the other into two strips and used the laces to tie it over his head like a bonnet while Mari did the same with Jess.

We were about three hundred meters out and I turned around to watch behind us while walking backwards. No posse yet but Franklin would be working on it. Nobody was crazy enough to plunge into the Scald unprepared. He would let us wear down then overtake us with a hundred men.

I didn't have time to ponder the coup and Harold's fate.

I was starting to hurt.

————————————

Five minutes later we heard the battle horn. Mari was beside me and glanced back every couple minutes. We were jogging and she slowed us to walk for a breather.

She pulled her scope and stopped to look while we kept walking.

If Father was in charge he would let us run ourselves out said Levi. Franklin is impulsive so will now endanger his men.

I think he had your Father's gun I said.

Father may have put him in charge. Or Franklin's men may have killed him. Father was wrong about the rapture; however it went wrong. So, he will be seen as a false prophet.

The heat was building fast. Mirage shimmers lay in the distance.

Does Franklin have many who will follow him? asked Mari, catching back up.

Only the worst of the lot. Those who want to abuse the people and seek new flesh supplies. Some like to hurt children.

What about Hoss? I said. I think he's the one who shot me.

He surely was. He is the best shot I've ever seen. He has always been with Father, but he's not to be trusted. I am sure Franklin has promised him and all that throw in gold and women. They see what has happened to Father but dared not risk anything before the rapture.

Why not just let us go? Mari asked. If Franklin can take over and your gone why come after us?

The people respect Levi said Jess. Franklin knows if Levi returns with the technology he can take power back. And many still believe the rapture will happen with my crucifixion, so he wants us both.

I had watched the Mission on the hill grow larger and the base of the sandy hill was now to our right. There was a mirror reflection from the Mission.

Mari look. The Mission.

She was looking at my bandage.

She stopped and pulled out the scope and we kept moving.

I look down and saw fresh blood on my shoulder.

Runners are coming she said as she caught up. And fast. He's put four up front and one has a gun. Annie is on the move through the Sage. Somebody in a duster is with her and I'm betting it's the guy who cut you down. Has to be the priest.

Priest? said Levi. He and Jess looked at each other.

Or Lucky I said.

Hold up everyone, she said. Levi cut me two more strips from the dress. Jess's dress was getting short now and exposing her bare legs to the scalding heat. She undid my bandage and quickly wrapped the new and pulled it even tighter. She kicked sand over the bloody one and felt my forehead. It felt hot but the rest of me felt cold. My system was diverting blood from extremities. She was trying not to look worried but I was starting to.

Lucky? said Levi.

Yeah said Mari. Lucky?

Long story. A movement caught my eye. Look I said. She looked up and followed my eyes to the hill. Somebody was coming down it.

She jerked the scope up.

Well there's something you don't see every day.

She turned the scope behind and found the runners. Then back up the hill to the plummeting figure that look like a man with a pole.

It's the priest. He's naked and has a cross on his chest that looks like blood. He's carrying a long pole with the Mission crucifix at the top. He's heading for the runners I would say.

Annie told him about Frida I said. She told him and he's going to buy us some time and die doing it.

We all watched. I handed Jess my canteen and told her just a little. She gave some to Levi. Mari and I took a sip and we just watched and waited, catching our breath. It was heading for a hotter than normal day.

Ok get moving I'll be right behind you she said.

We started walking slowly then picked it up to a fast walk. I saw something coming in high ahead of us. A drone I had never seen fly dropped down about ten feet overhead and we had some shade. Dr B and the J's had retrofitted a high flying fast drone we rarely used with Phantom hover drones. The big drone had broad wings like a mini fighter jet and put down a tight triangle of shade. We moved closer together into it.

That's your Father, Jess said Mari. He can see you.

She looked up and smiled.

I was taking our drone count and all we had left were over our head. I could hold up my canteen and Dr. B could probably get us some water by drone but we would lose our shade. I was trying to calculate how long it would take for it to fly back, get strapped with water, then fly back.

My head was a beating drum. Vision blurring. Put one foot in front of the other.

Jess I'm losing my vision and Levi isn't much better. Don't let Mari get out of our sight.

She turned and was walking backwards looking for her.

She's coming she said.

Mari caught up and was quiet, catching her breath.

Nice shade she said.

We ordered drinks but they're not here yet.

It was the priest she said. The runners saw him and stopped. Then they fled. Franklin and the posse are about a thousand meters back and they stopped. The Priest ran right into the middle of the posse. I couldn't see what happened, but the pole went down and so far, they're not moving. He bought us a lot of time.

Mari put an arm around my waist to help me walk. We were silent as we walked in the shadow of the drone, thinking about the priest.

Life Can Be a Drag Man

We had walked for two hours and I was struggling to stay conscious. Mari checked behind us every couple minutes. The posse had fallen back. Her and Levi were half-carrying me and Jess was struggling. Dr. B would send water and help when we were close enough.

I focused on one foot in front of the other.

The transcriptors were great at regulating body temps in a healthy body. But if traumatized the brain took over. My arms and legs were deep black while my core and upper torso were bright red. My body temp was not plummeting as the suit now worked like a blanket.

Our water situation wasn't good. Jess had been up all night and probably no sleep for several days. Being crucified does that too you. Levi had been beaten half to death. Mari would make it on her own, but trying to drag me was tempting fate.

Hold up I said. The shade drone went past then pulled back.

I knew I was about to become stupid or worse. I could barely see and breathing was shallow. I still had anxiety and the bleeding had slowed some which was good - but if lethargy started I was in big trouble. Hypovolemic shock could follow.

Can you see Annie I said.

Mari was already looking through the scope.

No. But the Sage juts out just ahead so that would be her entry point. It would take her about thirty minutes to reach us. Since she has a bad knee maybe a little longer.

Mari leave Levi and I here and take Jess. Dr. B will have somebody coming out. We will keep moving just slower.

Levi was nodding his head in agreement.

Oh hell no she said. We're not leaving anybody. We have to keep moving.

The Scald had picked a bad day to be hotter than usual. It was at least sixty celsius.

Mari was pale.

She put her lips against my forehead then took my head in both hands.

Annie will be there. She will have water.

She knew if we veered off to intercept Annie we were moving away from a straight line to the Church. If Annie didn't make it we were screwed. So, we would stay on the straight path and hope she came to us. And the guy in the duster. Lucky.

Jess...one foot in front of the other sweetie said Mari. You can do it. Your Dad has sent help. We are almost there.

She didn't respond but started moving. There wasn't much left of her white dress.

The next fifteen minutes took hours. Or maybe it was thirty minutes. I tried to focus and control my breathing and keep my pulse down. My limbic hadn't taken over but I was getting confused.

Hold up Mari said. Her voice was a little high pitched. I could tell. She was my girl. She was something.

Time went by. Levi was talking to me. I don't know what he's saying. He doesn't have a shirt. He likes Jess I think.

Lay him down I heard her say. Levi shouldn't lay down without a shirt. This sand is hot.

The back of my head on the sand. It was going to boil my brain. No there's a hand under it. I felt lips on my cheek. Someone had their hand over my neck. I think it was Jess. My feet seemed to be missing, we have to go back and look for them. The sky is like a big airplane I'm hanging from, but we're not moving. Weird. Someone is talking in my ear. Sweet Mari. She is whispering sweet things. What is she saying? I don't know but I can tell it's sweet. I really love that girl. When we get off this airplane I'm going to make love to her. Why isn't this thing moving? My eye is pulsing. My heart is in my eye. The airplane is breathing with me. Maybe we're getting ready to take off. What was that? Mari said love. I love you too. I think my lips are saying that. What is wrong with my lips? Someone is stroking my forehead. Now two voices. Jess? Is that you? What is that? I don't know what you're saying. You're going to have a bad sunburn. I have voices in each ear. Sweet voices. Maybe they are angels. Rebel Angels! That's funny. Fucking Hags. Where's my blade. Voices in stereo. They talk and talk back and forth and it goes on and on. Something cool on my forehead. That feels so good it almost hurts. Now my lips. Mari? No no its cold not like Mari she's warm. But it tastes good. She tastes good. That feels really good going down. I feel it falling through me. A waterfall. The voices are louder. Hands on my head and neck.

What is happening? I think they are strapping me in. This must be a fast airplane! I bet Dr. B built it. That's one smart dude. My legs are moving? I didn't order that. I'm moving. Someone grabbing me. I hope Mari has her blade out I can't find mine. More cool in my mouth. That feels so good. I wish I had water to go with this. We have to find some water soon. It's so hot out here. We're moving? The plane is finally moving. It needs to go higher I'm dragging on something. Who is that talking?

———————————

Cool breeze on my face. Eyes open to a whooshing bank tube. Breeze making them water. Mari smiling at me. So far so good.

She gave me water and kissed me while smoothing my burr. She smelled good. The Mood was on me. She was in a white T with green yoga pants. Nice.

I was going to ask how you feel she said. But I see what you're looking at. Dr B laughing behind me.

Is everyone ok? I managed to rasp out.

Dr. B kneeled beside Mari, hand on my arm.

Everyone's going to be ok my boy. Our super girl here was badly dehydrated but she's recovering fast, no surprise. Jess was the same and a nasty sunburn, but she'll be ok. Levi's pretty beat up but will be ok. He's very strong.

Annie?

144

His eyes started welling up.

She's good my boy. Better than good. Her knee is banged up but otherwise good. I owe you two everything.

Mari put her arm around him.

Sir none of us would be here if it wasn't for you and the J's. You saved us with the drone attack, then saved us again with the shade.

We should have put water on it somehow, he said. I'm sorry. We thought you would find more water before the Scald. And we were out of drones. We didn't want to leave you without shade.

No worries said Mari. There was no way to plan for all this. It was crazy.

I could hear a commotion outside our door.

"He's awake!" Soon the entire crew was crammed into our cubicle making a fuss and crying.

I tried to get up.

Hold on my boy said Annie. You need some more rest. We got you stitched up but you lost quite a bit of blood. Nasty neck scar but Mari said you should have a zipper on your neck anyway.

Everyone was laughing and it made me cough out a laugh.

She laid on the drag poles with you as we got close. She whispered things in your ear which must have been good because you were mumbling yeah that sounds good, yes let's do that.

Mari was blushing and hiding her eyes as the room broke up.

Good thing I'm wearing a titanium suit I said. She gave me a playful elbow as everyone howled. I noticed someone with a metallic nose was missing.

Did Lucky make it?

Yeah, he's downstairs trying to get Gabriel to eat.

No shit I said. More laughter.

And the Posse?

They trailed off then turned back.

That was curious.

Levi was in the door with Jess. His face wasn't as swollen but black and blue.

Levi what do you make of that?

I realized it was probably hard to talk with a battered jaw.

I think they got too far behind because of the priest and Franklin couldn't control the men. Nobody wants to chase the Devil across the Devil's playground when their families are back home in a bad situation. Their heart wasn't in it.

Do you think they will come looking?

No, I think they have enough problems in the town. Power struggle over who is the boss. Franklin and his boys will be looking to take control but Father has many old guard who won't have him as boss.

You need to rest said Annie. Mari has volunteered to be your nurse - imagine that.

Everyone was patting me and laughing. I really liked that sound.

Dr B was the last to leave and said he would make us some strong coffee in a bit and we could talk. I gave him a thumbs up.

Mari gave me a drink of water and crawled in beside me. Damn she felt good. It seemed like a year since I had felt her curled against me. She blew in my ear and giggled.

You were very naughty on the way back.

Sounds like you were too. And I meant every word of whatever I said.

She laughed and laid her head next to me.

I guess Annie knew to bring drag poles?

Yep. She saw the wrap around your neck and Levi limping so her and Lucky stripped two saplings down before hitting the Scald. We used Lucky's duster as a sling and he pulled you until Adam and James arrived. That's when I thought some dirty talk would keep you going.

You know me well my love. How long have I been out?

We got back noon yesterday. About twenty-four hours.

I knew from the portholes the hammer sun was high.

I was so scared she said. I'm not afraid of the whole Hag Nation, but seeing you like that...

It's ok baby. I was scared too. But I knew with you there I would make it. You're the greatest warrior there is.

She put her arm over my chest. I was happy to be alive and with my girl. We had saved Jess and Annie and come home heroes.

It was a holiday movie ending.

So why was something nagging me.

She fell asleep against me as I lay staring into the cool breeze of the bank tube.

———————————

The smell of coffee woke me. Mari woke with me as always. We just lay there quietly, syncing our breathing.

Dr. B peeked in then knocked. He had a fresh pot and set three tins on the table.

How are you feeling?

I was working my way into sitting up on the mat with Mari's help.

Foggy I said. But I have a good nurse.

He handed us both a steaming cup and pulled a chair from the table.

You probably shouldn't be drinking coffee yet but what the hell. He poured and handed us each a hot tin.

Sara is getting you both something to eat. Then maybe you'll feel up to coming to supper tonight.

I will be there I said. Maybe even tell some jokes.

We all had a sip. He made a strong cup.

Something's on your mind my boy.

I took another sip, enjoying the steam on my face. My Mood was calm black.

We got Jess and Annie. The Hags are in turmoil. Everybody's recovering…

But… he said.

I feel uneasy. I don't know why. Maybe it's just some post-traumatic stress.

Maybe he said. I would say being in a heightened alert state after that is normal. I also think it worries you the Hags turned back. It is strange. Once they set on a path it's do or die.

That turnabout does bother me I said. The priest bought us some time, but they could have overtaken us in the Scald. Mari was practically dragging us. They have scopes, they knew I was wounded. They knew Levi was hurt. And they had guns. They wouldn't test Mari's blade, but they know where to shoot us now. And at least one of them can pull off that shot with some consistency. And he's a sadistic little shit.

But I think Levi's theory makes sense said Mari. Franklin had to turn back because his men were more interested in what was happening behind them. Their wives and children left to fend for themselves in that chaos. A lot of them probably fled out the East gate and into the Sage. A really bad time to set off across the Scald in a posse. And they could see how bad you were bleeding, and didn't know Annie and Lucky would be helping us. They figured we would be buzzard bait by lunch.

You're right I said. And Levi knows better than anyone.

But there's something else I think, he said.

I glanced at the door, then lowered my voice.

We brought two Hags back. We may have put us all in grave danger.

Do you trust them?

I know how Levi looked at Jess when she was on that cross said Mari. And Franklin had betrayed him. They beat him nearly to death over it. We wouldn't have made it across the Scald without him. When Niki wanted us to leave them behind Levi agreed.

And Lucky saved us from crucifixion I said. I almost had an arm free but I don't think I was gonna make it before Franklin started driving a stake.

Why did he help you?

Well I cut his fingers off in the basement so got off on the wrong foot. But then I showed him something I don't think he had ever experienced. Kindness. I gave him a way out of that hell and he took it. We knew he had guts. But to come back into town and cut me down like that. Damn. I think he will be loyal to us for the rest of his life. And I agree with Mari. Levi knows his Father is near the end, either by insanity or at the hands of Franklin. If Franklin had driven those stakes into Jess…Levi would have killed him first chance he had if Harold was gone. Franklin knew that. I think he will be true to Jess and to us. And he's a big bad dude. And young. We've always known if Mari or I went down the Church would be vulnerable. And while my love here looks younger every day I'm getting a little long in the tooth for this sort of thing.

Please Mari said.

Dr. B laughed.

I never had a second thought about it he said. I trust your instincts without reservation. And Annie feels the same way. She watched Lucky trying to feed Gabriel at the well. She figured one of you had taken his fingers and sent him to the well for a reason. I think Gabriel is wary of him though. The metal nose.

We all were laughing.

You weren't kidding about Annie, sir. She is something else.

That she is kids. That she is.

We had never seen Dr. B this happy. His daughter, his wife, his family. Pure joy.

I set that nagging feeling aside.

We drank coffee and relaxed. Sara brought some fried yams and perch that was delicious. I complemented her and Adam on the chewy bars and how they got us through.

She laughed and said after we left she had one and was still picking her teeth.

Mari and I lounged around and listened to the sounds of the Church. Things were already falling back into the routine of daily life and it was comforting. I knew after a couple of weeks we would be getting antsy, an urge we would quell with hard training and scrounging. We treated scrounging like a treasure hunt, and it lent some flavor to the otherwise tedious days.

We loved our family dearly, but the bubble world was small.

The supper bell was clanging early and we were glad. I knew I had to be on the mend because I was starving.

Lawrence was setting out tin plates. I put my arm around him and he said he was feeling better. Just allergies. We had found him ten years ago on a scrounge, trying to survive in a burned-out building near a river, ten years old. He was emaciated, near starvation. He had never been able to talk about what happened to his family, and hadn't said a word for the first few years. One night at supper Mari filled his tin with some mashed potatoes and kissed the top of his head. He grabbed her arm as she turned and said thank you. We all cried.

Mari came over and hugged him and he blushed. He helped her and Sara with the fish while I watched the J's slice yams on the tabernacle. They always had a dialogue going, frequently over my head, but I was learning. Mari and I would often sit in on their conflabs with Dr. B about the possibilities of alien life finding us, time travel, gravity waves, and anything else that struck their fancy. Although the math was generally beyond us, we had come a long way. Dr. B told us he considered us grad students.

The J's were gregarious and fun loving and brilliant. Every problem was solvable. Dr. B would joke they had to be related to Feynman. As a boy Mom had given me a book by Feynman. It was about physics but also his life and just the world in general. It was funny and smart and I never forgot it. You can figure things out, if you have curiosity and pay attention to what *is* actually is. And have fun doing it.

Annie and Jess were making the rounds to see if anyone needed help. I thought of the hell Annie had been through for eighteen years, seeing her daughter who didn't know her, trying to mend horribly abused people. Yet here she was looking none the worse for wear. How does one keep the mind together through that? Every night, shivering on a dirty bedroll, hearing cries of misery. Eating unspeakable things. Knowing your daughter is just up the street in the house of the worst man alive. Not knowing if your husband is dead or alive.

The fish and yams were being dished out so the table filled up quick. Dr B sat at the head. Adam and James had rounded up some stools from the basement for our bigger family. Monique and Sara were fussing over my bandages but I told them it was ok - I was hungry so I must be almost well. They agreed that was a good sign.

A big plate of yams in the center of the table had a candle in it. Annie lit it and we sang happy birthday to Jess. Her and Levi had never heard it before but had big smiles. She blew her candle out to a big cheer. Annie and Dr. B. cried along with everyone else.

Adam had sentry duty and Hanna and James went up to take him a plate with some coffee. They seemed to want to go up together, so that was new since we had been gone. A crisis does bring people together.

I was gonna go up just before sundown to see him, and scratch that nagging itch a little.

Supper was warmth and laughter. Jess and Levi couldn't keep their hands off each other causing lots of smiling nudges and winks. James told everyone not to panic as the still was operational again which caused a loud cheer. I had two plates of fish and yams with what must have been a gallon of water. I had my girl, two doctors and a nurse watching me, so I had to do the right thing.

I remembered our little table on the Trinity river. This same feeling. My little sister would throw a piece of corn at me and giggle. I would eat it and say the corn monster thanks you! We would have our supper then sit on the porch talking and laughing. I would read at bedtime while Mom read to Sis. Dad would sit on the porch till late making sure we were alone on the river. He didn't sleep much for a lot of reasons.

I thought about Dad and his soldier instincts. He had witnessed the depths of human depravity, and could still be a loving Father and husband. But he never lost those instincts. He just shifted them to protecting his family. I thought maybe it was time to go see Adam.

Everyone was finishing up and cleaning the table. I asked Mari to fix another big plate for Adam and I would take it to him. She gave me a long look as she handed it to me. She knew I had an itch. She had the same one, but her total focus since we got back had been me.

Easy on the stairs she said.

Adam was thrilled at the heaping plate. Best yams ever he said. He asked how I was doing as I sipped a tin of coffee.

Doing pretty good my boy. I got back with my girl and my equipment so the future is bright.

He was trying not to get yam up his nose as he sputtered a laugh.

Dammit Niki I think I got yam up my nose! He laughed again and went back at his plate.

How does the Scald look tonight? Is it still sandy?

Yes sir. All seems well. I think just some coyotes moving about.

Before dark?

I'm not sure. I was scanning with the binoculars and thought I saw movement by the party barge. I watched for a long time though and didn't see anything. James told me he saw a couple coyotes hanging out around it last week, so that's probably what it was.

The wildlife has been asking strange I said.

Adam had a degree in biology and a general fascination with all living things. I told him what Mari and I had seen at the truck circle.

That is incredible sir. There have been many reported incidents of animals knowing when a natural disaster is coming. During the 2004 great tsunami dogs refused to run on the beach, and elephants were defying their handlers and trying to get to higher ground before the wave. Snakes and rats have been known to flee underground nests before earthquakes. Horses have also been known to be sensitive to impending events. Just how you described the wild ponies matter of fact. And bats and insects have infra-sonic hearing and are far more sensitive than us at knowing something's up.

I guess the next question is what's up.

Yes, but before that is why natural enemies are hanging out together. I've never heard of that on that scale.

Was Mari ok?

Yeah, she closed her eyes and I got her outta there.

Very good sir. What you and she did will be sung about around campfires someday.

Like ninety-nine bottles of beer on the wall?

He laughed.

You were part of it too my boy, I said. And let's just hope our little motley crew here can make someday happen.

Why don't you go downstairs for some social time? I'll keep an eye out.

Are you sure? You probably should be taking it easy.

That's what our medical staff keeps telling me. Look, I got that beat down chair I can relax in. I promise not to fall asleep. If I do the duct tape will keep me from falling out.

Yes sir he laughed. I will come back in a bit.

Get going I said with a pat on the back.

I plopped in the battered chair as he hurried down the stairs.

I rolled to the portholes and brought the binoculars up to see if I could spot some coyotes. Maybe even wolves. The sun was low and the Scald was turning hazy red.

I zeroed in on the party barge. It was far enough out to strain the binoculars to get any details.

When it sank, maybe 2025, people still had pleasure boats and the Scald was still a lake.   It hit bottom with one corner on a boulder and lay resting with a list towards us, creating a rare piece of shade on the backside. I imagine if we were to dig down a few feet on the low side we would find a lot of beer that went down with the ship.

The pontoon logs were facing away with the swimming deck facing us. It was not a huge barge, built for maybe ten. I focused along the bottom corners, looking for movement, odd shadows, anything different. I had scanned the wreck thousands of times.

It looked like it always did.

I scanned across the rest of the Scald and took a coffee break.

My neck was burning. Stamina sucked. Climbing the stairs was tiring. Just holding the binoculars for a few minutes had me down. The yam overload wasn't helping any.

I sipped to laughter from the kitchen. It would be dark soon. One more scan then trust Angel.

Like Levi said. The Hags had bigger problems in town. Harold might be dead. People would suffer even worse at the hands of Franklin.

Harold standing there staring at the drones when hell broke loose was nagging at me. Annie said he had dementia and he sure looked like it. But his prayer in the Square wasn't rambling or incoherent. The grand spectacle he had planned for the crucifixion and rapture was the old Harold - well planned and dramatic.

So, where was he? Why was he not with Franklin and that short shit who shot me?

I took another look at the barge. The sun was very low and the shadows were long. If anyone were in the shade there might be a shadow. I slowly scanned each corner, the bottom edge, the top of the rusty swimming deck, every square foot. Nothing was out of place.

The chair squeaked porthole to porthole as I scanned the rest of the horizon. I took a long look at our path coming in. Dr. B had sent Adam and James out this morning to cover the drag lines and drag new ones off towards the Sage. But the Hags were expert trackers. It was the only thing we could do but they could probably figure it out and come right to our doorstep if they wished. We had never fled Hagtown ever - much less in a straight line to the Church. I was hoping for high winds the next few days to cover our tracks.

We had the drones back in the air and no posse was moving. In fact, Hagtown seemed quieter than it should have been.

The power struggle in town was the only explanation. People afraid to come out.

I heard Mari's voice and knew she would be up soon. I spun the chair around to watch her come up the stairs. I would make her laugh squeaking the old beater in time with her steps. Out of the corner of my eye I saw the belly dancer.

What the hell, take a look.

I rolled to the center porthole on the north and zeroed in on the black funnel. I could hear Mari saying something to Hannah at the foot of the stairs. The belly dancer was fading into the dusk and flickers from the flame below were reflecting on the low black shelf cloud. I pulled back to scan the expanse of wasteland in between. The burned buildings and desolate streets receded with the belly dancer as I pulled back onto the north edge of the Scald.

Mari was coming up the stairs.

The Church set on the north shore of the former lake on a low hill. Down the hill heading into the city had been a narrow concrete road, winding a half mile or so into a bigger east-west road. The other side of the big road was a mist-mash of strip malls and fast food joints and billboards. Rusty steel skeletons rose from black piles, marking the ignominious end of a way of life.

I rolled the scroll and pulled back down the concrete road. There was an abandoned semi-truck trailer just off the big road. The rusty truck that had pulled the trailer was separated about thirty meters away. Mari and I figured the driver had dropped the trailer trying to flee and was pulled out. The driver's door hung open, sagging. The trailer behind it was wobbly and twisted with sheet metal that flopped in high winds. Both sat on rims that looked like rusty knobs.

Are you watching the belly dancer again baby?

I saw two birds take off from the top of the truck cab.

She came up behind me and rubbed my shoulders as I held the binoculars locked.

Hannah has a thing for James. He seems to like her as well. I hope so. I think they would be a good match. How are you feeling? I've never seen you eat that much. We may have to do a yamectomy on you.

Niki?

Baby what's wrong?

Sweetheart, go find Dr. B right now.

We have a problem.

Mari ran down the stairs.

I was thinking.

Her and Dr. B ran up the stairs with Annie not far behind.

What is it my boy?

I stood up and Mari put her arm around my waist. They could see it in my eyes.

Sir we have to make a plan and get ready. We are going to wake up at dawn surrounded by the Hag Army.

Annie gasped and put her hands over her mouth as Mari put her forehead on my shoulder. Dr. B closed his eyes for a long moment. It was that moment that had stretched into our lifetimes, when anything good was always too good to be true.

What did you see?

Two birds spooked from the old truck cab on the north road. A runner took off from behind the trailer heading west. And a damn big shadow remained that is not a coyote.

Dusk had turned into dark.

Do you think it's Harold?

Yes. I think there are other runners staged to the west that will relay a message back to town in a couple of hours.

That message will be Father has found the lair of the Rebel Angels, so march straight north through the night. He now knows we can see them with drones in the daylight. The moon will be out and he will tell them to just follow the tire fire. He will meet them before dawn and surround us.

The great man's brows were furrowed in thought.

Annie would you go find the J's please he said.

I think I know how he did this said Mari. He knew from those three dead mopes at the East gate we had sent Annie up to the Mission, but didn't care because Jesus was coming. When we lit out across the Scald I was focused on watching the posse to the south and Annie to the east. Nicki was neck-shot and looking straight ahead, while Levi could barely see.

When the runners turned back because of the priest, he took them and circled around to the west I said. The posse was a decoy. He knows a posse can't take us down. He had to find our hiding place and Dr. B and bring his whole damn army.

He could have stayed way out and tracked the shade drone I said. He would send runners ahead to keep sight. Either he or a runner saw us disappear into the Church. Harold knew we would be watching south, so he set up north behind the trailer where he could see us coming and going. If he had waited five more minutes I never would have seen the runner.

And if he has Annie's pendant there is no guesswork about us said Mari.

How many do you think will march? asked Dr. B.

Fifteen hundred at least. He wants the army to see this, but can't leave the town unprotected either. Franklin will be in charge of the march. And it seems likely somebody in that group has the pendant. Harold or Franklin are the heavy favorites.

But they still have the same problem they've always had said Mari. They have to take it on faith we are in a Church they can't see. They've just had their faith shaken when the Rebel Angels took the Virgin and prevented the rapture. And they have to know Harold has lost his mind.

So, we have to shake their faith some more said Dr. B.

Annie came back with the J's. I could hear voices in the sanctuary so the trouble vibe was spreading.

Annie, I said. I hate to do this after the beautiful day we've all had. But can you huddle everyone around the table again and we'll be down in a few minutes.

She hurried back down.

I have an idea I said. But I need to know if it is technically possible. If it is then maybe our little congregation has a chance.

———————

Everyone was gathered around the table, looking very anxious. All of our lives had been this sort of emotional roller coaster, from calm to fight-or-flight in a heartbeat.

We are going to be ok said Dr. B. But we have a situation that is going to unfold at dawn. We have all night to prepare. I need everyone to do exactly as I ask you. I need everyone to help prepare three days rations and water. Then go to your cubicle, get dressed and prepare your backpacks to leave.

Several gasps at the word leave.

Stay calm now - I said prepare to leave. When you are dressed and packed everyone will go to the basement. Niki, Mari and Levi will stay up here.

He had his arm around Jess. He whispered something to her as she wiped away a tear.

Listen everyone. I'm not going to tell you what is happening at dawn. I need you to trust me. Trust me because I trust our three warriors. And Angel. You have to have faith in their power. You saw what they did in Hagtown. So, get started now, and know everything will be ok.

There was burst of scooting chairs as the plan went into motion. We had about seven hours.

––––––––––––

I headed back to the sentry room with Mari and Dr. B. Levi was talking to Jess and I asked him to come up when he was done. I told her it would be alright.

Mari was in the chair scanning the Scald, listening to Dr. B.

The J's are going over the drones he said. We will have one in the sanctuary and one in the front up high. Lucky will be at the basement door and Annie will relay messages to me if we lose a drone.

Levi came up the stairs a little slower than I had hoped.

How is your leg? I asked.

It's ok he said. Just stiff. Father wouldn't have beaten me so badly but he gave the task to Franklin. He wants me dead. He swung his hammer at my thigh. It glanced but bruised badly. It would have shattered my leg. Father pulled him back.

Your brother's a real asshole I said.

Yes. He's not my real brother. Harold just picked the kids he thought would be the strongest. We never got along. His real Father was a youth minister. Mine I never knew.

If this plan doesn't work you will be the most vulnerable I said. He will make an example of you.

I know. I just want Jess to make it out with her family. With all of her family. Warriors expect to die in battle.

I was glad we brought him back.

Lucky came up and took the chair and binoculars. He would be on lookout all night, holding the binoculars with his good hand. If I was right they would start tightening the circle just before dawn. At sunup Harold would be at the spot he saw us disappear. The front door to the Church. If he had the pendant even better.

Dr. B went down to help the J's. Mari and I kneeled either side of Lucky to watch.

Thank you for what you did back there I said. I think we would have died without you.

I thought you were almost out of that strap he said, keeping his eyes on the Scald while smiling under his metallic nose. But a little help couldn't hurt. We got lucky with the ladder. It was hard to balance since I only have one hand now.

Sorry. I did leave your thumb.

He laughed.

Are you really a Muslim? There is some debate around here about that.

No. But my Father was. And some of the people in town had known him. One day coming back from gathering I kneeled to help a wounded bird. I was kneeling the way I had always knelt with my Father, just out of habit. Unfortunately, I was facing east. A son-of-a-bitch who was coveting my wife ran to Pat and told him I was Isis. That's what they call them. When Pat found out about my Father he hauled me to Harold and next thing I knew I was on the chopping block.

And they wouldn't eat Muslim Mari said.

That's right he laughed, still scanning. His voice had a nasal twang from the metal nose.

I didn't want my wife to be chopped after me, which they would have done after passing her around the soldiers. So, I had to do something dramatic. Dramatic displays of pain are the only thing that impress Harold. I guess because of Jesus on the cross and all that. So, I hacked off my nose and that really impressed him. It hurt like holy hell let me tell you. Annie kept me from bleeding to death and had someone make this robot nose for me.

So you're not a believer? I asked.

Hell no. I was like a lot of people in that town, just going along to get along. We ran out of options you know? Play along or get tortured and eaten. I never understood why my Dad believed what he did, or why Harold believes what he does. I didn't want to care. I just wanted to be left alone to not believe.

Did anyone really believe the rapture was coming? Mari asked.

Some. Those at the foot of the stage are devout, most others thought Harold had just lost it. We could see his eyes had gone crazy. But honestly, I think the sight of you two probably made believers out of everyone. You did look like demons.

That was the idea I said. And when we get the chance we will find your wife.

Mari and I headed down to our cubicle. Lucky would come get us if he saw anything. Dr. B was huddled with Levi.

We held each other for a long time.

Didn't we just do this a couple of days ago? She mumbled into my chest.

Seems like a year ago I said.

She took a deep breath.

How is your energy? You up to this? I know you were more exhausted than you let on. You're still a little pale.

I'm yammed up she said.

I made a pot of coffee and set a candle in the middle of the table. We looked through the tiny flicker and discussed the contingency plan. There would be no failure but if there was something that didn't look like victory always have a backup plan.

We did a pinkie swear that if one of us didn't make it the other would soldier on. We knew the importance of the survival of this motley congregation but didn't go there.

In my deepest heart, I didn't think I could go on without her. Her eyes said the same thing.

Just one more time. Just one more victory.

———————————

Two hours before dawn Lucky told Dr B they were coming.
 Everyone went to the basement and Mari and I suited up in the vestibule. We went up and told Lucky to head down, leaving only Dr. B and Levi.

We took turns watching. They weren't moving but we saw the glints of moonlight on steel and crosses. Glints that formed a circle around the Church at the edge of sight.

With one hour left Dr. B went to the basement.

We headed down to the vestibule while Levi watched.

We stood in the vestibule, Moods red and ready, helmets down. My exhaustion was drenched in adrenalin. My neck hurt but I didn't care. Mari was ready. She had that look in her eye.

She went to the back of the sanctuary and I opened the big doors wide. Dawn was beginning to peak. I could see the soldier circle in the distance.

Levi came down the stairs. They are moving. Father is in lead with Franklin on his right. This is most of the soldiers Nik. The circle is complete.

I nodded and he went back up.

Mari was in the shadows shimmering red. I gave her the thumbs up.

Harold was marching towards the door. That was good. About two hundred meters out he veered off course. Franklin pushed him back on course with a stiff arm.

Now that was interesting. And perfect.

I moved to the side of the door as they closed the circle. Mari watched from the shadows with a scope. The hammer sun was about up and heat was building. The bank tube overhead was whooshing cool air but I couldn't feel it. My heart felt like it was in my neck. The sound of two thousand men marching at us. Harold coming to our doorstep. That was good.

The ring of soldiers marched about twenty meters behind Harold. They began chanting.

Jesus is our sword…Jesus is our sword…Jesus is our sword.

They banged blade handle on hammer after every sword.

I knew they could hear this in the basement. Probably feel it. I hoped they stayed calm.

The marching stopped.

Rebel Angels! he boomed.

Your trickery was great and deceived me once. But I'm only a man! My heart was not right with God almighty and I was punished.

But I set it right with the Lord!

A roar and clanging of steel.

The power of Jesus once resided in my two boys. One fell to Satan. The other stands beside me. God has given him the vision! He can see through the Devil's tricks!

Another roar. You have a choice Rebel Angels. Send out your leader. Send out the great man. If you send him to me, you will all live. You will live as citizens of Hagtown. I give you my word. If you do not obey me, with the power of Franklin's vision I will have these soldiers of God descend upon you.

Everything went quiet. I closed my eyes and drew a deep breath. I could smell them.

Now Rebel Angels. Do it now. Do it now or the time for you to die is nigh.

I stepped into the doorway and Franklin smiled.

He stands before you Father! The Rebel Angel!

And then I saw it.

Hanging from that stupid green cross was Annie's heart. The pederast could see us and didn't have any idea why.

With a dramatic flair out up and over Harold raised his blade, pointing towards what he guessed was the cross. Franklin adjusted his arm a little. His big crucifix and chain were gone. He wore the crucifix from the Mission hanging from an old rope, framed by his loop of teeth.

Step aside demon! Step aside and send out the great man.

Instead I stepped out of the Church and took three strides toward him.

I emerged from the laser halfway between Harold and the door. The soldiers let out a cry as I appeared. More clanging of steel.

I was staring at Harold.

We said the great man demon! screamed Franklin. I stared at Harold, ignoring the pederast.

The great man is impressed by your skill mighty Father I said.

He asks for mercy. The technology has blinded him. It has blinded us all. But clearly your God is greater. Clearly you are his champion. He asks that you take my head as an offering, and spare the rest, who will accept Jesus into their hearts.

I looked at the sky and closed my eyes.

I kneeled before the giant.

I bowed my head and stared at the sand as a huge victory roar erupted from the horde.

Time slowed.

My neck was throbbing. I could smell the horde, their gaping maws reeking of decay. Sweat-soaked leather and piss.

Let us pray my soldiers of God! Harold boomed.

The horde fell silent.

I kept my head down. A grain of sand pulled my eyes into its sameness. I thought of William Blake and saw a world.

We have smote thine enemies oh mighty Jehovah!

Amen!

With your divine wisdom, we have rooted out the evil!

Amen!

With your divine eye, we have seen through the Devil's tricks!

Amen!

With your divine power, we will now cast this Rebel Angel into the fire!

Amen!

I could hear footsteps on the stone.

The horde let loose their blood lust.

Slay the Rebel Angel! Take his head! Take his head!

The blue laser rolled across the tiny worlds in the sand.

The horde fell silent.

The footsteps grew quicker and I braced elbow on knee.

A sudden impact on my shoulder blade, pushing me down, then gone.

As my body recoiled I looked up to see Mari flying out of the blue, blade cocked high. Out of the blue her body flew, the new sun shimmering her blazing red. Her shining blade was slashing across as she descended. Harold stood with mouth open.

The blade struck like lightning.

Slicing the old rope, severing the leather tooth loop, deep into his throat and out the other side, slinging blood as it cleared.

Blood poured from his open neck in a torrent of life. He drew a final gasp, the wound gurgling in blood and air like a drain into hell. The Mission crucifix was falling, trailing rope and teeth and torrents of red. It stabbed into the Scald to the knees of Jesus, showered with teeth and drenched in blood.

Harold dropped to his knees and collapsed onto the crucifix, face in the sand, dead.

The ring of soldiers stood in silent disbelief.

Mari landed looking at Franklin. As Harold shook the earth hitting the sand, I whipped a blade blurring past her helmet. It pierced his bulging eye with a thud of the hilt on his skull, death coming at the very moment he saw his Father and Faith die.

The force of the blade jerked his head back towards the sky, hilt pointing towards the heavens, his body about to realize it was over. Mari slid the point of her dripping red blade under the pendant as he fell backwards. His body popped the necklace and the heart slid down her blade, trailing blood. As the pederast fell dead in the sand the heart hit her hand.

The blue laser flashed over us as Mari came to stand beside me, facing the horde.

The silence turned into hysteria, soldiers sobbing, pulling their hair in anguish and despair, on their knees pounding the sand.

The laser now disappeared just as fast. They could see us, see the Church, see it all.

They all stopped to stare up at the cross on the Church.

They started backing away, dropping their hammers and blades, staring at the cross.

A booming voice from above stopped them.

Soldiers! Listen to me now!

Levi was atop the dome, one arm holding onto the cross, the other pointing his blade at the sky.

You will return to your homes. Take care of your wives and children. I will come for you soon, and the truth shall be revealed.

It sounded like a commandment from God.

The soldiers were overwhelmed.

Shouts of Levi!   He will save us!

The blue laser flashed back and we were gone and the exodus of the horde back to Hagtown began in mass, leaving Harold and Franklin pooled in red and dead in the hammer sun.

_____

I heard Levi yelling all clear and the basement emptied. Mari had her arm around my waist as mine draped her shoulder. They rushed out the door towards us before seeing Harold and Franklin.

Levi stayed back with Jess, keeping her turned away from it. She was frantically telling him something.

We herded everyone back in the Church and shut the doors.

We had been closer to the abyss than ever.

We shook their faith up didn't we sir? Your timing was flawless.

It required great courage and skill to work my boy.

And leaping ability I said, squeezing Mari. I'm hope someone is going rub this bruise on my back.

I was thinking about Levi's commandment.

Levi, we will help you. With those two dead, maybe the suffering can stop. I don't know how but we will help them. We will have to act fast. They will expect your return and maybe the soldiers can hold things together, but that short shit will be rabble rousing, looking to take control. He may be half Harold's size but his heart is just as big with hate.

I know you wouldn't leave them to die he said. But Jess said we won't have to. We won't have to go back.

I don't understand I said, looking down at Mari then at Dr. B.

Everyone suddenly grew quiet. They were looking at us with a strange look, but smiling.

The great man spoke.

Something has happened kids. Something I believe I would have to call a miracle.

Mari squeezed against me.

We won't need to go back to Hagtown, he said.

It seems there will be a rapture after all.

Copyright